A Passionate Love

The Bennett Triplets

Delaney Diamond

Chapter One

"Woo hoo!"

Simone Brooks smiled and shook her head as she watched her older sister, Ella, lift a glass filled with a brightly-colored liquid to the sky and shake her butt to a techno beat in front of the deejay. The way she was kicking up her heels and letting loose, one would think it was Ella's party and not Simone's friend Kim's divorce party.

Divorce parties were all the rage now, and Simone had attended quite a few—the last one taking place as recently as two months ago in Cabo—which turned into a three-day weekend where her friend started out partying and flirting with strange men, and ended with drunken, sobbing pleas for a reconciliation on the phone to her ex. They'd had to wrestle her to the ground and yank away the phone. The ugliness of regret was not a pretty sight.

Sipping her French martini, Simone scanned the rooftop.

At least this particular party was a one-night affair, held at Club Masquerade, a popular Atlanta nightclub. VIP waitresses wearing purple and green masquerade masks weaved between the guests standing around or seated on the wicker sofas and armchairs filled with colorful cushions, and assembled around the low tables and portable fire pits. The design mirrored a living room, giving guests the opportunity to gather close and chat and eat in a cozy atmosphere.

The fifty or so partygoers, many of whom Simone didn't recognize, seemed to be enjoying themselves. But why wouldn't they? Her assistant, Adele, had organized the affair, and Adele knew how to throw a party. With Simone covering the cost of the festivities to ensure her friend had a good time, they'd purchased the most expensive VIP option Masquerade had to offer.

The package included a plush suite at the Loews Hotel a few blocks away for Kim, and a chauffeured stretch SUV for her and her closest friends. When they had arrived, two hostesses greeted the core group of ten at the door and promised a night of "mayhem and good times." They hadn't stopped partying since.

Ella danced over, clutching a Planter's Punch, eyes overly bright, and wearing one of the biggest smiles Simone had ever seen. Clearly she needed this night away from her kids.

"Are you having *fu-un?*" Ella asked.

"Clearly, you are," Simone said with amusement.

"I am. I so needed this." Ella closed her eyes and swayed to the beat.

A strand of hair had come undone from the tight bun she typically kept it in. Simone smoothed the hair back into place, certain it would fall free again once Ella went back to full on dancing.

"Have you tried one of these?" Ella popped a fried morsel of food into her mouth.

Simone shook her head. "I'm not hungry."

"They're really good. They're called beer-battered broccoli bites. Mmm. Between them and the teriyaki chicken skewers, I'm in heaven." She did a little wiggle.

Yeah, she was definitely enjoying herself.

Simone should be, too, and should have eaten instead of only indulging in the strong, free-flowing drinks mixed by the bartender. The menu options here had a good reputation, one of the reasons she'd settled on this location from the list of options her assistant had provided, but she didn't have much of an appetite.

She set her drink on the low wall and briefly wished she didn't have to be at the party, smiling and excited about Kim's divorce. As far as she was concerned, a divorce was nothing to celebrate. There was too much pain and heartache involved in the dissolution of a marriage. A wedding should be celebrated, but she was beginning to think she'd never be one of the lucky ones to have that type of celebration.

She grimaced as the throbbing headache and queasiness in her stomach surged to new heights.

"Hey, are you okay?" Ella asked. Concern filled her eyes.

"I'm fine," Simone lied. The ache of loneliness lodged in her chest.

Her sister's hand came to rest on her right shoulder. "Are you sure you're okay? You don't look so good."

"Actually, I feel a little nauseous." Simone rubbed her belly.

"Have you eaten anything at all?" Ella asked.

"No, I haven't."

"Drinking on an empty stomach is not good."

"I know." Simone pulled in a breath.

She had moved from Seattle to Atlanta a few months ago. As a philanthropic ambassador for the family's Johnson Foundation, one of the largest private charitable foundations in the world, she did important, meaningful work on a daily basis. Yet she remained unfulfilled. Disappointment and frustration were constant companions since her last breakup only weeks before the move.

Thirty years old and back to square one.

"I'm going to find a bathroom," she said.

"It's out the door and to the right," Ella said. "Hurry back."

Simone smiled wanly at her sister. "I will."

She didn't really have to use the bathroom. She just wanted to get away from the loud music and laughter for a few minutes.

It was darker inside the club, and with the dance floor a couple of floors below, the music was not as loud. Only the distant beat of a hip hop song could be heard as blue, purple, and red strobe lights flashed across the ceiling.

A wave of dizziness hit and Simone placed a steadying hand to the wall. Groaning inwardly, she reluctantly admitted her sister was right. She shouldn't have been drinking on an empty stomach. Maybe she should find the bathroom. Moving along the carpeted hall with slow, careful steps, she dragged her hand along the wall, eyes searching for the restroom sign.

Up ahead a man stood near one of the pillars, wearing a dark brown suit, forearms on the balustrade, head bouncing to the music as he surveyed the action below.

Simone paused.

She couldn't see his face. Craning her neck to get a better look in the dimly lit interior, she only saw the back of his closely shorn head and the height and shape of his body. He was a big guy, with a wide neck and broad shoulders.

Inexplicably, her heart began to race. She blinked a few times and quietly circled behind him.

Now she could see his profile, and had a good look at a strong jaw. Her heartbeat quadrupled, pounding so fast she placed a restraining hand against her chest. What the heck was wrong with her?

She continued to move, silently cursing when she staggered. She shook her head briskly to clear the dizziness, but doing so only worsened the disorienting feeling and she flailed her hands to regain balance.

The movement caught the stranger's eye, and he turned suddenly. Simone managed to face him, legs spread apart to keep her balance. She placed a hand to her queasy stomach.

He left the railing and came toward her, his face furrowed in concern. "Ma'am, are you okay?"

"I..." She couldn't even talk, and he remained silent, giving her ample opportunity to fully examine him.

He looked like an African god dropped into modern society, wearing a chocolate suit and matching tie. Even under the conservative attire, she could tell he had a firm body. All man, he was easily six foot three. He had a dark brown complexion, as if he'd been dipped in maple syrup, a beautifully broad nose, and lips so thick and luscious-looking they were downright indecent.

Dark brown eyes scoured her frame, dragging down the length of her body with the same intense inspection she gave him. His right eyebrow lifted a fraction higher over his eyes, and her nerve endings heightened at the attention, the hairs on her arms standing on end.

"Ma'am, are you okay?"

The sound of his voice again—deep and decadent as the finest chocolate—made her insides tremble.

Opening her mouth to speak, Simone flayed her hands in a flustered, inane movement that affirmed how rattled she was by him. Finally, she regained control of her limbs and pointed up. "I-I'm at the rooftop party."

He nodded his understanding. "Oh, you're a guest at the divorce party?"

"I'm throwing the party for one of my friends."

"Oh." He came forward, his smile friendly, its brilliance rivaling the colorful strobe lights that crisscrossed the ceiling. "I'm one of the owners of Club Masquerade. I hope you've been enjoying yourself."

Simone wanted to say what a good time they were having, and how pleased she was with the service they'd received so far. She opened her mouth to speak those very words, but they didn't come.

The building nausea chose that very moment to make its presence known in a horribly embarrassing way. Instead of words issuing from her mouth, the liquid contents of her stomach bubbled up and spewed from her lips—all over his black shoes.

Chapter Two

Cameron poured tepid water from a bottle he kept on his desk into a crystal tumbler and handed it to Simone. At least now he knew her name.

After he escorted her through the doorway to the offices in an exclusive part of the club, she'd cleaned up in his private bathroom. She now sat in one of four purple and gold chairs arranged in a semicircle behind an oval coffee table in front of his desk. In the quiet office, she cupped the glass in both hands, her manicured nails touching each other, and drank gratefully. When she had drained every drop, she set the glass carefully on the table before her, the faint outline of her plump lips remaining on the edge.

"I'm terribly sorry about your clothes."

"You don't have to keep apologizing. Things happen."

It could have been worse. At least the contents of her stomach were all liquid. He had been able to clean his shoes in the bathroom but couldn't do much about the edge of his pants leg. Luckily, he'd picked up his navy blue suit from the cleaners on the way to work, and it had been hanging in the closet in his office. With the addition of a blue and pink striped tie, he once again appeared presentable.

"Well, they don't happen to me."

Folding his arms across his chest, he asked, "What happened this time? Couldn't hold your liquor?"

"I can hold my liquor just fine, thank you," she said primly.

"I was kidding," he said with a grin.

"Oh." She returned the smile, a little hesitantly at first, and then visibly relaxed, laughing—perhaps at herself. "I guess I should be a little nicer to you, considering what happened."

She used perfect diction, all proper and somehow sexy. Her long hair hung in loose waves past her shoulders. Thick and silky-looking, it gleamed under the recessed lights in his office and framed her round face, which was a welcoming canvas of full, nude lips and dimples.

"I suppose you have to get back to work," she said.

She stood in one controlled, graceful movement, a spectacular image standing in front of the wall-sized windows. He usually liked women who wore less clothes and exuded overt sexuality, but the chic, elegant outfit showed off her great figure without appearing lewd or immodest. The burgundy pencil skirt brought attention to her hips and narrow waist, while the navy blue shirt clung to her torso, hints of chestnut skin appearing beneath the lacy design.

"Well, Mr. Bennett, if you—"

"Cameron."

The interruption threw her and she paused. "Very well. If you—"

"Say it."

Her eyes widened. "Excuse me?"

"Say my name."

His neck tightened, and tension thickened in the room. She parted her lips and then quickly closed them again. Then she frowned, as if she intended to refuse, but instead cleared her throat. "Cameron."

The hairs on the back of his neck straightened. Her tone was quietly inviting. Almost as if she was seducing him with the way she said his name. He knew he was staring when her gaze jerked away from his, but he couldn't help himself.

Simone cleared her throat again and smoothed a hand down her skirt. "As I was saying, I'd be happy to take care of having your suit cleaned. I'll have my assistant give you a call tomorrow sometime and we'll take care of it."

"Is that the best you can do?" Cameron asked.

Her back straightened, and her eyes narrowed on him. "Mr. Bennett—"

"Cameron."

She took a deep breath. "Cameron."

The same reaction. Goosebumps on his skin, just by the sound of his name on her tongue.

"Please tell me you're not trying to extort money from me simply because I'm well-off."

"I think we both know you're much better than 'well-off.'"

His sister, Harper, oversaw all of the club's special events, and she'd told him the group had spent an exorbitant amount of money, purchasing the gold package with all the extras—bottle service, hostesses, the works. No expense had been spared, and he didn't doubt for one minute that chauffeured cars, private planes, and extravagant parties were all part of a normal day for someone like Simone Brooks.

Yet he couldn't fight the urge to get closer to her, even as he considered that she was way out of his league.

"I'm not interested in a dry-cleaning service. I'd like to take you out," Cameron said.

Simone licked her lips, and the movement moistened her full mouth, prompting him to envision them lying together and sharing sweet, hungry kisses.

"Take me out? I don't think so."

"Why not? Something wrong with me?" He spread his arms, giving her a good look at the full length of his body.

"I—"

Warmth filled his chest at the way her concentrated gaze seemed to examine every aspect of his body. No doubt about it, she was just as attracted to him as he was to her.

"There's nothing wrong with you. Unfortunately, I recently moved back to Atlanta. I'm getting reacquainted with living in the south again, not to mention I'm extremely busy with a new position and all its responsibilities. I'm sorry." She clasped her hands before her. "I'm not interested."

"So you're telling me that in between the reacquainting and learning the ropes of a new job, you don't have time to sit down and have dinner. I find that hard to believe."

"I don't have a lot of spare time."

"Hmm…considering you threw up on my favorite suit, I think the least you could do is make the time to join me for dinner," Cameron said.

"No, the least I could do is pay for your dry-cleaning," Simone said.

Spunky. He liked that.

"We're at an impasse, but you know what the right thing is to do," he said.

"Let me guess. I should accept your offer for dinner."

"Exactly."

He grinned, and after a few seconds she fought a smile of her own before she gave up the battle and the corners of her mouth turned up, and those cute dimples in her cheeks made an appearance.

"Is this what you do regularly? You run one of the hottest nightclubs in Atlanta and pick and choose from the droves of women who come in here every night? It's quite the racket you have going."

"Actually, Club Masquerade is not one of the hottest nightclubs in Atlanta, it's the hottest in the city."

"Oh, I stand corrected."

"And only very special ladies get my attention."

"So I'm special, is that it?"

He was silent for a moment, watching her closely before he answered. "I believe you're very special, Simone Brooks."

Her lips separated in a silent gasp, and she quickly lowered her gaze, hiding her expression, but not before an indefinable emotion leapt to life in the depths of her eyes. He couldn't explain it, but he suspected his words not only surprised her, she needed to hear them.

Strange. Why would a woman so put together—chic, wealthy, and beautiful all in one package—have need to hear that she was special?

"It's just dinner," he said quietly.

She lifted her gaze, studying him with dark brown eyes that were decidedly more guarded than before.

"Dinner it is," she agreed.

Cameron curtailed the urge to punch his fist in the air, instead taking a pen from the cup on his desk and removing a small notebook from the inside breast pocket of his suit. "What's your number?"

"I can enter the digits into your cell phone," Simone offered.

"I don't own a cell phone."

She cocked her head to one side. "What did you say?"

"You heard me."

"Please explain to me why, in this day and age, you don't have a cell phone."

"I don't need to have a cell phone when everyone else has one."

Cell phones were a modern convenience he considered a blessing and a curse. The way he figured, if anyone needed him, they could find him at the club or at home. Otherwise, they could leave a message. Seldom had he experienced a situation where someone actually really needed to reach him right away. The freedom of not having an electronic device glued to his face every single day was a relief. He gave his up years ago and didn't miss it.

"Number?" Cameron poised the pen above the lined paper.

Simone shook her head, as if she couldn't believe him, and then gave him her number.

"This is your real number, correct? Because we do have your contact information on file."

"You have my assistant's contact information on file, but yes, that's a good number."

"Perfect. I'll call you. That way you can pay your debt."

She opened her mouth to speak again, probably to make a tart reply. Seeming to think better of it, she pursed her lips, and gave a little laugh before walking toward the door.

He followed, watching the way her body moved, his nostrils flaring at her sexy, hip-swinging walk. He bit his knuckle. Goddamn.

She turned at the door and looked back at him, her hair swinging in a thick wave between her shoulders.

"Have a good evening, Mr.—Cameron."

"You too, Simone."

When the door closed behind her, Cameron expelled the air from his lungs in a huff and sat on the desk, gripping the edge.

"Wow," he murmured.

Chapter Three

Back on the rooftop, Simone found her purse and touched up her face, reapplying her lipstick and dabbing a bit of powder on her nose and cheeks.

When she was finished, Ella approached. "What happened to you?" her sister asked.

"Nothing." Aside from the mortification of throwing up on a complete stranger, she felt much better than when she left. Lighter. Almost giddy.

Avoiding her sister's shrewd gaze, she walked over to the table of heavy hors d'oeuvres and plucked a piece of beer-battered broccoli from a platter. The crunchy shell crackled in her mouth. She chewed and swallowed the tasty appetizer, a hint of sweet and spicy hitting the back of her throat.

"I don't believe you," Ella said behind her.

"What do you think happened?" Simone asked.

"I don't know, but you're going to tell me." Ella took Simone by the arm and tugged her over to a far corner against her will, away from the deejay where they could speak without yelling. Ella placed a fist on her hip. "You came back with a smirk on your face. What's going on?"

Simone laughed. "There's nothing to tell."

Ella's perfectly arched brow lifted higher. "*Simone.*"

Her voice took on their mother's stern tone, and Simone almost laughed at the similarity. Like their mother, Ella wore her hair in a neat bun. Wearing a tight mini that showed off her almost-back-to-pre-pregnancy-weight figure, she still appeared conservative. She even looked like their mother, with her narrow face and high cheekbones.

Simone sighed heavily and rolled her eyes. It was futile to avoid her sister's questions. Ella wouldn't stop until she'd wrung the answer she wanted right out of her. "I met the owner of the club. His name is Cameron Bennett."

"So?"

"He…asked me out, and I accepted."

"You just got back into town and you're jumping into another relationship?"

Simone bristled at her sister's tone. "First of all, I'm an adult. Second of all, I'm not entering into another relationship. We're going to dinner."

"Why? He's the owner of a nightclub."

"Don't be a snob. Besides, I owe him."

"What could you possibly owe him?"

Simone launched into an explanation of how she'd thrown up on him and then the conversation in his office.

"Sounds like he's a slick one," Ella said drily.

"I can handle him." Simone waved away the concern and walked over to the railing. As usual, Peachtree Street was alive with cars and pedestrians, as if residents would rather be out and about—anywhere but at home. She was the opposite.

As a member of the wealthy Johnson family, whose multibillion-dollar beer and restaurant empire was run from their Seattle headquarters, there was always some function to attend, particularly in her line of work. Her mother, Sylvie Johnson, was a sister to the now-deceased head of the Johnson family and a brilliant businesswoman in her own right, who managed a personal portfolio of successful businesses and investments.

Simone steered clear of the business aspects of the family fortune and concentrated her efforts on promoting the Johnson Foundation's causes. That was her strength.

She'd moved to Seattle five years ago to work more closely with the foundation, concentrating her fundraising efforts on issues surrounding children's causes in housing, education, and healthcare. When her relationship ended, she decided to move back to Atlanta and take on a more active role in the charitable giving arena.

In her role as philanthropic ambassador, she was a volunteer but did have an expense account. Her busy social calendar included international travel and representing the family at events around the country. Fundraisers, volunteering on benefit committees, and schmoozing with other socialites at the theatre and charity balls all fell under her list of duties.

The family's generous donations made a huge difference in the lives of the beneficiaries, but so much of her work included attending parties, Simone looked forward to quiet evenings at home. Rather than visiting the hottest nightspots, relaxing in front of the TV or having people over for dinner was her favorite way to engage with friends and family.

Ella came to stand beside Simone. She remained silent for a while, as if sifting through her thoughts to find the right words. "I hate to say it, but this guy…Cameron, is that his name? He could be like all the others."

Because of her acute attraction to him, Simone didn't want to think about that possibility, but her sister was right. Cameron was not from their world, and she'd seen often enough the fallout when men couldn't handle women with her type of wealth.

The Brooks women didn't have much luck in the love department. They were either jinxed or simply unlovable.

Only months after her last child was born, Ella's husband, an executive at the Johnson family restaurant group, left her. Long before that, at the age of fifteen, Simone and Ella's father divorced their mother, Sylvie, after a contentious marriage, leaving her to be a single mother to two boys and two girls.

Simone gnawed the corner of her lip, flipping over the conversation with Cameron in her mind. "We'll go out to dinner, have a little fun, and that's it. I'm not taking him too seriously."

"So you say," Ella said skeptically.

"Don't be so negative." Simone bumped her sister's shoulder with her own. "I'm not looking for forever, and it'll be nice to have someone to go out with. You don't exactly have time for me. You're busy with the kids, and Reese and Spencer are always chasing women." Ella groaned in agreement about their brothers. "It'll be nice to have someone to spend time with when I'm not working and traveling."

"Make sure he's not married."

"Oh my goodness, you're the worst, you know that? He's not."

"How do you know?"

"He wasn't wearing a ring."

"That doesn't mean anything. Make sure."

Simone stared down at the gleaming diamond and emerald ring on her right hand. He wasn't married. Not only did she not see a ring on his finger, there were no family photos in his office. In all honesty, she didn't think he was the type to hide that he was married.

She was certain of it. She just *knew.*

Quietly, she asked, "Do you think you'll ever get married again?"

"No way!"

Simone glanced at her sister, whose eyes followed the line of cars below, jaw set hard in resolve. Simone looped an arm around her sister's and leaned her head against her shoulder. Ella had been very hurt when her husband left, and Simone's heart ached from knowing that her sister had suffered such an abrupt and unforeseen end to her marriage.

"It's not worth it, Simone," Ella said softly, her voice vibrating with pain. "Have fun, but guard your heart."

Simone nodded, unable to talk over the lump of emotion stuck in her throat.

Was this really who she had become? A guarded thirty-year-old woman who focused solely on her work at the foundation, and closed off so no one could get near enough to hurt her? That wasn't the life she wanted to live, but it seemed that was the future spread out before her.

Cameron's handsome face and brilliant smile came to mind. With a smile like that, he had to be fun, and he was certainly pleasant to look at.

If dinner went well, he could be her interim dating partner. Until Mr. Right came along.

****

A floor manager sidled up beside Cameron as he stood on the second floor overlooking the jostling crowd. A stocky woman with a cheerful demeanor, Stella oversaw the kitchen on the first floor.

"I thought you were leaving early," she said.

"I had some things to take care of." He angled his body in her direction, watching the colorful lights flash across her light brown face.

Stella pulled a pen from behind her ear. "Since you're here, mind signing off on this order for me?" She extended a clipboard.

"Hank signs off on the orders," Cameron pointed out, referring to the assistant general manager, his second in command.

"I know, but I couldn't find him, and since you're right here, I thought I'd bug my super-duper, wonderful, generous boss instead."

She smiled brightly, and a half smile crossed Cameron's lips in response.

"What do you want?" he asked, not falling for the extra compliments.

"Um, any chance I can have next weekend off?"

He heard the hesitation in her voice, and rightly so. He had no problem with staff who needed a night off here and there outside of their regular schedule, but with weekend nights being the busiest, the club maintained a strict policy that if staff wanted an entire weekend off, they were required to put in the request at least two weeks in advance.

Cameron looked up from the list of supplies. "The whole weekend?"

Stella nodded, biting her lip.

"I'm not going to tell you no, but you know the rules." He perused the first page of the supply order and flipped to the next page. "Have you talked to Hank?"

"I was kind of hoping—"

"You were hoping I'd say yes and override him." He scribbled his signature on the last page and handed Stella the clipboard. "Hank is your direct supervisor."

Her face sobered. "I know."

"You should always go through him, and that's what you need to do this time. Talk to him. Make sure he has coverage for that night. If so, I have no problem with you taking off the weekend."

"Thanks, Cameron."

She hurried away.

"Hey, Stella."

She stopped and turned slowly, clutching the clipboard. Trepidation marred her features, as if she was worried he would pull back his permission.

"Talk to Leticia. She mentioned wanting to pick up extra shifts."

Stella's shoulders sagged in relief and the smile returned. "I will!"

After she'd left him alone, Cameron turned his attention to the swarm of people gathered around the circular bar. Men and women waved cash in an effort to catch the eyes of the busy bartenders, while others took advantage of the bar stools, crowded close together and flirting as they sipped their drinks.

His brother, Mason, monitored the inside and outside of the club from a security office on the second floor, but he also liked to keep an eye on the goings on. The combination of a large crowd and alcohol could sometimes take a violent turn, and every extra pair of eyes was valuable.

His eyes focused on two men shoving each other and jockeying for position, but the altercation quickly died down when a thick-necked bouncer dressed in a black suit intervened.

Cameron hadn't only stuck around to keep an eye on the club goers. His gaze shifted to the escalator, where patrons glided to the first floor. He was watching—waiting, for another glimpse of Simone.

He laughed at himself. What was he doing? She and her friends could be here all night, and here he was sticking around for one last glimpse of her.

Shaking his head in disgust, he pushed away from the railing, but something on the escalator—or rather *someone* on the escalator, caught his eye.

He froze, the muscles in his abdomen tightening.

Simone and a small group of women descended, talking animatedly to each other. The same feeling he'd experienced upstairs—a breathlessness, like an asthmatic would suffer—clenched his chest.

And all he could do was watch.

The women wound their way through the crowd, turning heads as they did, and a few feet from the exit, Simone turned. As if she knew he was watching.

A muscle in his jaw tightened as they locked eyes. Cameron didn't turn away or hide his blatant observation.

Simone hesitated, and they remained transfixed, each with their eyes fastened on the other.

She truly was an attractive woman. She waved, and he smiled, lifting a hand in greeting.

One of the women with her, whose hair was in a neat bun, followed Simone's gaze and seeing him, looped an arm through Simone's and tugged her toward the exit, breaking the spell.

Cameron kept an eye on the back of Simone's head until she disappeared.

Devoid of her presence, it was as if a dark cloud descended over the club. He no longer saw the flashing lights. He no longer heard the thumping music.

He remained rooted to the spot a few minutes longer, eyes trained on the entryway she'd disappeared through.

What was wrong with him?

Cursing silently, Cameron shook his head vigorously and snapped out of the trance.

Then he walked away to make his own exit out of the club.

Chapter Four

She was either late or not coming.

Cars whizzed by on the busy street where Cameron paced the sidewalk in front of Cooks Gadget Warehouse. Checking his watch again, he huffed in annoyance, as if that would make Simone appear.

Sunday nights were his night off, and he'd scheduled their date at the gourmet store where he purchased cookware and other kitchen supplies. It also served as a cooking school. Staff teachers and guest chefs taught almost every night of the week, and he'd booked a class during couples' night for him and Simone to attend. Tonight's menu consisted of a two-course meal, made up of an appetizer and entree, but if Simone didn't appear within the next few minutes, she'd miss the beginning of the two-hour class.

When he'd called her to set up a time for their date and get a sense of what she liked to eat, he'd learned that she didn't cook. At all. Before he hung up, he knew he wanted to bring her here. Cooking was a creative way for them to get to know each other. Something different, at least, since he was pretty sure nothing he suggested could compare to dates she'd had in the past.

Unfortunately, she'd clearly stood him up.

Fighting back the urge to slam a frustrated fist into the red brick exterior, Cameron spun around and entered the store. He would not let her absence spoil the night. Walking through the retail space, he nodded at the young man who looked up from a recipe book behind the counter, going all the way to the back, where two stations were set up on either side of four ranges.

He went to his assigned spot where he shared a range with a tall, blond male and a South Asian woman with a red bindi on her forehead.

"Hi," Cameron said, and they returned the greeting.

He checked inventory against the items on the ingredients list, making sure he had everything to prepare the dishes. Tonight's meal started with a prosciutto-wrapped grilled fig salad and ended with lamb and beef stuffed ravioli in a spinach-cream sauce.

The instructor, a stout woman with her hair braided into two chunky cornrows, came by. "Alone tonight?" she asked.

"Seems that way." He donned an apron and tugged the strings tight with unnecessary force.

"You'll be fine. You should be teaching the class." She winked at him and went to check on other students.

Chuckling to himself at the compliment, Cameron set out glass ramekins and a cutting board for the *mise en place* prep. It was second nature to get all the ingredients laid out beforehand, something he'd been doing ever since he started cooking with his father at nine years old.

His father once advised a young Cameron that, *"Everybody says the way to a man's heart is through his stomach. I'm here to tell you, that's the way to a woman's heart, too."* Then he winked. *"That's how I got your mother."*

Cameron hadn't understood the importance of those words back then because he'd only been interested in the opposite sex if he could tug their braids or snap a bra strap. Working in the kitchen was strictly about the cooking and creating a dish that others could enjoy. Even in the midst of playing kickball or softball with neighborhood friends, Cameron often found a way to join his father in the kitchen.

Once he got older, the skills he learned served him well, paving the pathway to the hearts—and beds—of many young women. His passion for cooking eventually led to a career in restaurant and hospitality management, where he worked for years before taking over his parents' nightclub with his siblings three years ago.

Thirty minutes into the class, Cameron had placed the fresh pasta for the ravioli aside to rest, when the click-clack of heels on tile caused him to lift his gaze from the counter. Simone strutted down the middle of the room like a runway model, looking completely unruffled in a black-belted orange dress with three-quarter length sleeves. A black Fendi Peekaboo hung in the crook of her arm, and the only reason he knew anything about the expensive purse was because his sister, Harper, had shown him a picture and gushed about it the week before.

"I'm here." She plunked the purse on the counter. Those weren't exactly the words he expected to hear. She made it sound as if he should be grateful she'd arrived at all. And to his chagrin, that's exactly how he felt.

Grateful. Relieved.

"I said seven o'clock."

"I know, but I got busy. Since you have no cell phone, I couldn't call you."

Cameron didn't miss the snide undertone in the last sentence. "Was that comment meant to diss me?"

"Absolutely not."

She opened wide, guileless eyes, and the next thing he knew, the corners of his mouth were twitching in a fight to keep from smiling.

"I thought you'd stood me up."

"I couldn't possibly do that. I owe you, remember? You made that very clear." Behind the very proper speech was a sarcastic sense of humor.

"All right, smart ass. Get an apron and let's get to work."

She gave him a saucy salute. "Yes, sir."

They dived into meal prep. Well, at least Cameron did. Halfway through chopping onions, Simone stopped to send a text. Two minutes later when the instructor advised them to prepare the ground beef and lamb, Simone wandered into a corner to speak privately into her phone. When the phone chimed for the third time, Cameron had had enough. He snatched the diamond-encrusted device off the counter, turned it off, and shoved it into his pants pocket.

Her mouth fell open. "Hey, you can't take my phone!"

The couple at the station next to them looked over at the outburst.

Bending close to her ear, Cameron inhaled the muted sent of a flowery fragrance that tickled his nostrils and made him want to press his nose against her skin. "I just did."

"Give it back," she said through tight lips and in a lower tone. "That's a Boucheron-designed phone. I don't want to lose it."

"I don't care if it was made by the Queen of England. You're not getting it back."

20

"I have important things to take care of." Angry eyes challenged him.

Unbelievable.

Standing with his feet set apart, Cameron crossed his arms and met her glower with one of his own. "Is someone you know dying?"

She blinked. "No."

"Is someone you know in labor?"

Simone sighed. "No."

"Then what's so important you can't spare me another hour of your undivided attention? We're on a date. You owe me, remember?"

She opened her mouth and he quirked a brow, daring her to argue.

She set her mouth in a mutinous pout before muttering, "Fine. I'm all yours."

His heart jumped. That was the plan—to make her his.

"What do you want me to do?" Simone asked, completely unaware of the inner turmoil caused by her flippant remark.

"Make yourself useful and wash the spinach."

With a final glare from the corner of her eye, Simone turned to the sink in a huff. She emptied the spinach into a bowl and turned on the faucet.

Cameron didn't say another word to her, and they set about making dinner.

Chapter Five

It wasn't that bad.

Although upset by the way he took her phone, Simone secretly tingled at Cameron's take charge attitude. He even impressed her with such an unusual date choice.

Most men would have tried to do something a bit grander or extravagant, like an expensive meal somewhere. Or, like one man did, hire a helicopter to fly them over the city. She had been impressed, but the trip hadn't been conducive to talking and getting to know each other. Even worse, when her date turned green from motion sickness, they were forced to cut the ride short.

"Now add your olive oil and butter to the saucepan and sauté the onions and garlic," the instructor said from the front of the class.

Cameron poured olive oil into the pan and handed two ramekins with the vegetables to Simone.

She took the dishes, uncertain what to do with them. "Just dump them in?" she asked hesitantly, keeping her voice low so no one else could hear.

"Yes. Add the butter first and stir them, so they cook evenly." His face softened, offering encouragement. At least he didn't seem annoyed anymore.

Simone added the butter and let it melt, and then dumped in the vegetables and stirred, and the scent of onions and garlic filled the kitchen as all around them, their kitchen mates did the same. Students at each station worked diligently, cutting, chopping, and stirring.

She smiled to herself, feeling silly, but liking the activity. Cooking! Simone was cooking and actually enjoying it. She'd have to let her housekeeper know. Martha would definitely get a good laugh out of that.

Head bent, Cameron chopped spinach for the cream sauce with swift but even strokes. He moved around the kitchen in a more fluid and graceful manner than one would expect for a man his size. The light blue sleeves of his shirt were pushed up almost to his elbows, the tendons in his forearms bunching and flexing as he sliced through the greens with precision.

The teacher came by to check on them but quickly moved along, spending more time assisting the other students.

"You must cook a lot," Simone said.

"It's one of my favorite pastimes, along with doing anything outdoors. Hiking, jogging, whitewater rafting—those are my loves."

"I can tell."

One of his eyebrows lifted high. "What does that mean?"

"I can tell. You know, you look…fit."

Her gaze skimmed the biceps hinted at under his sleeves, the wide trunk of his body, and lean waist. When she brought her eyes back to his, he was watching her with a little smile on his face.

"Yeah?" he said. A flirtatious smile crossed his lips.

"Yeah." Simone bit the corner of her lip and returned her attention to the pan, stirring furiously. Cameron made her feel unbalanced. She never got off balance.

He leaned close and she went still, tensing.

"You look pretty fit yourself. Your legs look amazing in those heels," he whispered. Then he slid away and went back to work.

Meanwhile, her skin tingled where his breath brushed her ear and sent ripples of excitement scampering down the side of her neck. She'd wondered if her attraction to him in their first meeting was a fluke. Apparently not.

"So what do you like to do in your spare time?" Cameron asked, scooping spinach into a bowl.

"I prefer staying in, watching movies." Simone shrugged.

"Oh come on, that's all? You don't like to do anything else?"

The teasing note in his voice encouraged her to open up. "Well, I love to ski," she said, venturing a look at him to gauge his reaction. He appeared interested, and didn't seem to have jumped to the conclusion that she was being pretentious or showing off.

"Where do you go to ski?" Wholly interested in the conversation, he turned in her direction with curious eyes.

"I've skied all over. There are excellent spots in Colorado, Canada, and Switzerland, but my favorite is the Sella Ronda circuit in Italy. They don't have the best snow, but it's a great place to ski, and there's this beautiful hidden valley at Lagazuoi with frozen waterfalls and majestic mountains on either side. Oh, it's gorgeous. Worth the trip for that alone."

"Sounds nice. Maybe I'll get to see it sometime."

"Do you ski?"

"No."

"You have to learn to ski first," she teased.

"Are you offering to teach me?" That little smile again, across his decadent lips. Did he have any idea how sexy that smile was? He must, because he wielded it often, like a weapon against her.

"If you're willing to learn, I'm willing to teach."

"That means you'll have to see more of me."

Simone lifted one shoulder in a casual shrug. "That wouldn't be so bad." Her heart raced a little faster as she awaited his answer.

Cameron's eyelids lowered to half-mast. "Nah, that wouldn't be so bad at all. We have a deal," he said.

They smiled at each other and then went back to work. Cameron was very patient, pointing out the liquid measuring cup they needed to measure two cups of heavy cream, and answering questions she suspected were pretty basic but he never made her feel foolish for asking.

They worked well together. While he took the lead, she worked beside him as a sous chef and made sure their station stayed clean as they went along, wiping down the counters and removing pots and utensils once they'd been used.

"How long have you and your siblings been running Club Masquerade? I don't remember that club when I used to live here before."

Cameron came to stand beside her and peered into the pan. His hip touched hers, and the mouth-watering aroma of the food was replaced by the mouth-watering scent of his skin and cologne. Over the course of the evening they brushed against each other a few times, but standing so close, lined up and touching, made the breath tremble from her lungs at the intense warmth that bathed the entire right side of her body.

"Club Masquerade has been around for a while, but under a different name. It used to be Club Zenith and owned by my parents."

He told her the story about how he'd worked as a general manager of a restaurant in a popular chain. After a personal issue with a higher up, he left.

"That was three years ago, and around the same time, my parents told me and my siblings that they planned to sell the club. Revenue had declined over the years, they didn't know what to do to turn things around, and weren't interested in investing any more money into it."

He continued to say he had seen an opportunity to finally run his own business and have the autonomy he'd secretly craved. He convinced his brother and sister to take over the club with him. They invested in new technology, changed the decor, improved marketing, and expanded the events business by inviting celebrities to have album release parties and other events there.

Another bold step was to serve gourmet meals at the club. He'd wanted a diverse menu, and to be known not only for a party atmosphere, but excellent food. To do so, they'd hired away a chef from one of the most popular restaurants in South Carolina to cook Southern cuisine with a modern twist.

"I work closely with the chef, and a few of my recipes have made it onto the menu. My pineapple and hibiscus cocktail is popular, and so are the beer-battered broccoli bites."

"I ate broccoli bites at the divorce party. They were delicious."

"That was all me, sweetheart." He grinned. "Anyway, we renamed the nightclub Club Masquerade, and it's now the most popular nightclub in Atlanta, where the motto is, 'If it's not happening at Club Masquerade, it's not happening.' And the rest, as they say, is history."

"Your parents must be very proud," Simone said.

"They are, and happily retired." He glanced down at the saucepan. "It's ready."

He took over and added the spinach leaves. While they wilted in the hot liquid, he explained that he was the eldest of a set of triplets, and they were all very close. Working together had only brought them closer.

She told him about her older sister, Ella, and her two younger brothers, and that her parents had divorced when she was fifteen.

"That must have been rough," Cameron said.

"It was, but it was rougher on my mother."

"She didn't want the divorce?"

"No."

Her mother, a strong, self-composed businesswoman, cried for days after her husband left, eventually escaping to Ecuador where she owned a home. She stayed for a week, and when she returned, the woman she was today had emerged—harder and more determined than ever to prove to her ex-husband and the world that she was self-sufficient and didn't need him.

The cooked ravioli went into the pan next, and Cameron tossed the pasta in the succulent-smelling sauce, topping off the entire dish with freshly grated Parmesan cheese.

Simone's mouth watered at the aroma emitting from the saucepan. With the dish finished, Cameron scooped the meal onto two plates, and Simone set about plating the salads.

"What about your father?" he asked.

"He lives in Florida, and from what I can tell, he's very happy that he's single. He and Mother…let's just say they fought a lot."

"Sometimes people get together and they're not compatible. It's better to be apart than to fight," Cameron said. "My parents were lucky to find each other. They celebrate two anniversaries every year. This year they'll celebrate forty years as a couple and thirty-six years of marriage."

"That's wonderful." Simone could only hope to find that kind of longevity in a relationship one day. As she arranged the salads on the plate and topped them with prosciutto-wrapped figs, she glanced sideways at Cameron.

"Are you looking for a perfect relationship like that, Cameron?" She asked the question lightly, but was overly interested in the answer.

He laughed. "My parents' relationship isn't perfect."

"Celebrating forty years together sounds pretty perfect to me."

"They have their problems, but…I guess their love for each other is stronger than the problems. They just work through whatever comes up." Cameron picked up the two plates of food. "Come on, let's eat."

Simone grabbed the salads and followed.

Chapter Six

Dinner had been great. The salad had been a good starter to the ravioli, which had been cooked to perfection. Now it was time to go their separate ways.

Outside the store, Simone and Cameron said goodbye to their classmates, who waved as they wandered off to their cars at the back of the building. When they were all alone, Simone fell quiet, wondering what to do next. Cameron had stuffed his hands into his pockets and looked off into the distance.

The lights inside the storefront went out, turning the spot where they stood even darker.

Simone cleared her throat. "Well…my obligation to you is over. I should call my driver, but you still have my phone." She'd been halfway through the meal, talking and laughing at a four-top with the couple they'd worked beside, before she remembered he still held her phone.

Cameron didn't move, and she sensed that he didn't really want to leave any more than she did.

"So if I don't give back your phone, you can't call your driver?" A mischievous glint entered his eyes.

"That's right."

"Huh." He rolled onto the balls of his feet.

"You're not planning to keep me hostage, are you?" She tilted her chin in fake indignation.

"Not quite."

"Then what did you have in mind?"

He stroked his jaw. "Well, you know, we didn't have dessert."

"No we didn't. A meal like that definitely deserves dessert."

"I was hoping you'd say that." He grinned, such a sexy smile and one that filled her chest cavity with warmth.

Simone wasn't just attracted to Cameron. She felt completely at ease with him—her mind at rest in a way that didn't usually occur when she first started dating other men. Usually there was an awkward stage where she tried to get a feel for their personality, and they tried to get a feel for her. While there was a bit of that, she recognized that she was way more relaxed. Playful, teasing, open with him.

She once heard a comedian say that when you first start dating someone, you meet their "representative." Only later do you get to know the real person. But Simone suspected that was not the case with him. This was the real Cameron and not his representative. This smiling, friendly, cooking man was the same person today that she would know six months from now. Six years from now.

Her heart tripped over the fact that she was thinking that far in advance about him.

Before she could fully examine her thoughts, Cameron said, "I know where we can get some great tiramisu."

"Where?"

"My place."

He answered with aplomb, as if his home were a well-known restaurant.

Pulse rate spiking, Simone played along with his game. "You made it?"

"Not this time. I picked up a nice hunk from a bakery that makes the best desserts." He kissed his fingertips. "It's absolutely delicious."

"That good?"

"It's criminal."

"Says who?"

"Everybody."

Simone giggled. "With an endorsement like that, I have to try it."

He looked at her then. Really looked at her. While she couldn't discern his thoughts, Simone guessed he was making his own internal assessment of her.

"You have to come to my house to do that. So what do you say? You want to get some dessert?"

There was much more to the question than the surface, and when he extended his hand, Simone hesitated for three seconds before taking it.

His hand swallowed hers, and sparks flew across her nerves, igniting her skin. They both tightened their fingers at the same time. He must have felt it, too. A strong attraction, a sizzling chemistry blatantly on display since the moment they met.

Simone looked down at their joined hands and the way hers fit perfectly in his, as if made to be held by him. Cameron pulled her in closer so that they almost touched.

"You ready?" he asked in a low voice.

She nodded. She was ready, for whatever would come next.

They headed down the sidewalk toward the parking lot and walked the entire way like that—hand in hand, without saying another word to each other.

****

Cameron parked his gray pearl Lexus GX SUV at the side of the building. Simone hadn't said much during the ride over, and he wondered if it was nerves, or excitement like he felt. His skin damn near thrummed with anticipation.

They exited the vehicle and walked to the brick building located in historic Old Fourth Ward, a thriving neighborhood located east of Atlanta. The diverse neighborhood was known for being the birthplace of Dr. Martin Luther King, Jr., and experienced an economic downturn in the sixties. In recent years, a resurgence had occurred, resulting in a growing artistic community and flourishing small businesses. Developers took great pains to preserve its heritage, even while they converted abandoned buildings into loft living for a demographic of young professionals and entrepreneurs.

A little over a year ago, Cameron moved into the neighborhood after living with a roommate for two years. They'd gotten along well enough, but sharing a living space with another person had simply been a means by which to save a nice nest egg and purchase a comfortable bachelor pad in a hot part of town. He bought the property as a foreclosure and the value had already doubled in the short time since he'd moved in.

They took the elevator up to his floor, where he led Simone into the huge open loft space.

"This is nice," she breathed. Her heels clicked on the walnut wood flooring as she walked deeper into the boundaryless room.

"The units sell fast here. This one was a foreclosure, so I've been slowly making changes."

Exposed brick and cedar beams in the sixteen-foot-high ceiling added character to the property and had been one of the many features that attracted him to the unit, but he'd had to strip and refinish the floors and remodel the kitchen with a brand of high-end appliances he preferred.

White curtains flanked either side of a window to the left—a window that was ten feet high and let in plenty of light throughout most of the day. Directly in front of them was a sitting area made up of two clean but old sofas and a chair arranged around a heavy mahogany table, all scavenged from his parents' house when they downsized after retirement.

"I haven't had time to go furniture shopping yet," he explained.

He'd brought other women here before and never cared what they thought. Hell, they mostly went straight up to the bedroom anyway. But a little part of him wanted to impress Simone. The old, comfy sofas and chair no longer seemed good enough.

She looked over her shoulder. "You have a terrace," she said with excitement. She dropped the Fendi bag on the coffee table and rushed over to the window.

Cameron had placed an iron patio set made up of a round table and two chairs out there. He spent the occasional quiet evening sitting out on the patio eating dinner, watching the sun go down. On his day off, it was the perfect spot for relaxing and sipping a beer.

Simone turned, lifting her eyes to the second level bedroom and the space below it, decorated with only a chair, desk, and lamp where he worked when not at the club.

"I like this."

"I still have some work to do, but it's home."

She walked over to his record player against the wall and the collection of records housed in six crates around it. He could watch her walk all day and night.

"Records and a record player?" she said, quirking a brow at him.

He didn't own one of those sleek, modern ones that integrated with Bluetooth technology. His was vintage, purchased for a pittance at a garage sale.

"Don't knock it 'til you try it."

One of his favorite things to do was go to the record store and browse the stacks. Not only did he find other enthusiasts with whom he talked shop, but many unknown artists in the vinyl age made great music. When the digital age came along, they didn't all make the leap, and countless times he'd found hidden gems to add to his collection.

"I'm not knocking your old records, but surely you've heard of music streaming services. They're all the rage now," she quipped.

"Oh, so you got jokes."

"I'm just saying."

She shrugged with one shoulder and sent him a cute little smile before diving back into the collection. The way she angled her body over the crates made him tilt his head and imagine what he could do to her once he got her naked.

"You're a blues man. I see the old greats—B.B. King, Muddy Waters, Robert Johnson. Wow." She continued flipping. "And names I don't recognize. Do you only listen to blues?"

"Mostly blues. Some old rock, disco, etcetera. Everything's all mixed in," Cameron replied, his gaze trailing down the curve in her spine, over her bottom, and lower to her shapely calves.

"No cell phone. An old record player and records. You're an old soul, Cameron Bennett."

He lifted his gaze to hers and laughed. "You say I'm an old soul. My family says I'm stubborn."

"Well, they know you better than I do. Are you stubborn?"

"Pretty much. I like what I like, and I'm not easily distracted by every new and shiny thing."

"That's a good trait to have," she said quietly. "Mind if I put on one of the records?"

"Not at all."

She pulled one of the disks from its sleeve and placed it on the turntable. The sound of an electric guitar crackled through the old speakers as "Rock Me Baby," by B.B. King started.

"That's good music right there," Cameron said.

He left her and went into the kitchen, where steel dominated the decor. Light glinted off the steel appliances and steel built-in shelves that took the place of cabinets and exposed his collection of dishes.

He set the last of the tiramisu on a plate, added a fork, and rejoined Simone in the living room. Her eyes lit up when she saw the dessert. "Where's yours?" she asked.

Chuckling, Cameron cut a slice with the fork. "There isn't much left, so we'll have to share."

He extended the fork and she pulled the scrumptious dessert between her full lips. His stomach tightened.

"Mmm."

Cameron cut another slice and ate it. Over and over, he alternated by cutting a slice, extending it to her, and then cutting off a piece for himself to eat. All the while, King's gravelly voice serenaded them with "Rock Me Baby."

When they finished the cake, Simone brushed a crumb from the corner of her mouth and licked her lips.

He was two seconds away from ripping her clothes off. Watching her take slice after slice of cake between her red, parted lips had to be one of the most sensuous things he'd ever seen.

She kept looking at him, as if waiting for something, and that's when he realized she was waiting for him to make a move.

As the album segued into the sultrier, edgier "Blue Shadows," Cameron took Simone's hand and drew her closer, barely managing to temper the urgency beating through his blood.

"So how was it?" he asked.

"Delicious," she said softly, sounding a little breathless. "You were right, it was criminally good." She licked her lips again, and this time he knew she'd done it on purpose. "But I have a feeling that tiramisu wasn't the only reason you invited me here tonight."

One corner of Cameron's mouth ticked upward. "I have a feeling you knew that when you accepted my invitation."

His finger touched the pulse hammering at the base of her throat, and she inhaled. Her breasts lifted and stayed as she held her breath. Cameron lowered his head to the same spot and she arched her throat. When his tongue swept across the hollow between her collarbones, she released the breath as a trembling exhalation.

While B.B. King bewailed how it felt to be alone, Cameron encircled Simone's waist with one arm and pulled her flush against his body. Cupping her face with the other hand, he went in for the kiss.

Their mouths meshed together. Slow and easy. Her lips softened beneath his, and he pried them apart to trace the edges with his tongue. She tasted sweet like the dessert they'd consumed—mascarpone cheese, amaretto, and cocoa—and his blood surged as he delved deeper into the kiss.

Simone moaned, leaning into him, and his fingers climbed into her thick hair. Angling his head, he kissed her harder, with fiercer pressure and ardent strokes of his tongue.

Drawn again to the perfumed hollow at the base of her throat, he showered kisses down the side of her neck. Her little mewl of pleasure echoed in his loins, and he pushed her against the wall, kissing her harder and more thoroughly, stroking into every corner of her mouth.

His awakening body hardened, and he lifted her high. In response, her arms immediately encircled his neck and held him tight.

Cameron turned off the phonograph and plunged the room in quiet. Moving through the house, he headed to the stairs, Simone's mouth traveling over his face and neck, her breathing irregular, her heart thudding against his chest.

Then with slow, careful steps, he started climbing up the stairs.

Chapter Seven

Cameron sat naked on the bed, his tight body even more magnificent than Simone had realized. Taut muscles extended over every surface of his deep-brown skin. His thighs, thick and sturdy as wooden planks were powerful-looking and sprinkled with fine hairs. Nestled between his hips, his heavy manhood stood proud and erect, making her loins ache and throb with anticipation.

She pulled the dress over her head and let it crumble in a heap at her feet. Her toes sank into the plush beige rug that covered half the floor as she stood before him, unselfconscious in a black lace bra and matching cheeky. Reaching behind, she unhooked the bra while Cameron peeled the panty down her hips. With her entire body exposed, his eyes lowered to where a narrow strip of hair covered her shaved privates.

He watched her with a rigid jaw and such heat in his eyes, her skin prickled everywhere his gaze landed. His hands cupped her hips and she almost sighed from relief, anticipatory trembling overtaking her limbs as desire seeped into her bones.

"You're a goddess," he murmured, tugging her onto his lap so she straddled him.

He cupped the back of her head, his fingers a little rough, contracting in her hair as he dragged her neck to his mouth and kissed her chin, jaw, and shoulders. His moist mouth on her skin felt so good she moaned, delicious sensations swirling through her lower stomach and making her ache. Gripping his broad back, she flattened her breasts into his chest, rubbing her nipples against the friction of hair so they thrust into even harder points.

With ease he moved them higher on the bed and rolled Simone beneath him, then kissed her breasts and sucked the chocolate caps like pieces of candy. She twisted against the intense pleasure, her toes tangling in the rumpled sheets.

"Cam…"

Heartlessly, he continued the assault, circling her nipples with his tongue, nipping the flesh with his teeth until she had no choice but to arch deeper into his mouth and whisper his name in a pained, helpless moan. He kissed down over her stomach and she watched him go lower. Taking his time. Savoring her taste. Alternating between licking and sucking as he edged closer to the most sensitive part of her body.

He nipped at her hips and flicked his gaze up. Their eyes locked before he pressed his mouth to the juncture of her thighs.

Simone jerked and a harsh breath hissed through her teeth. She became one big pulsing ache of need, and extremely sensitive to his touch.

His hands slid between the mattress and her ass to cup her bottom. Then he truly went to work between her legs. His tongue and lips made love to her clit. Gentle tugs and quick strokes prodded her closer to the edge. She fought the urge to slam her thighs around his head but lifted her hips higher, gasping, eyes shuttering closed under the stimulating pleasure of his mouth.

Cameron squeezed her ass, his tongue continuing to glide across her sensitive skin. Seconds later, she succumbed to the urge of release. It was embarrassing how quickly she came.

Her mind went blank and she cried out, shuddering through an orgasm of epic proportion that surged through her blood and forced every muscle to tighten and seize. Her thighs gave up the fight and clamped around his head, and her back arched off the mattress as she rode out the storm.

When he finished, a cocky grin swept one side of Cameron's mouth. He swiped a hand across his glistening lips and reached to the nightstand beside the bed. He slipped on a condom and positioned himself above her, kissing the corner of her mouth and giving her right breast a quick tug with his lips before gripping her hips.

With one smooth thrust the full weight of him came between her legs, and Simone clamped her arms around his neck, anxious for more contact.

He filled her body, pressing into her—hard, warm, powerful.

She sighed into his neck. Pure, unadulterated completion filled her being. This was where she belonged. With this man, in this bed.

Cameron pulled back and lunged forward again with one long thrust. He groaned. "Damn. You have the sweetest…" The words ended on another rough-edged groan.

With her bottom nestled in his hands, he moved with slow, measured strokes. Skin to skin, they rocked. Slowly, he increased the tempo, and she followed suit until the strain of a pending orgasm built in her loins.

As if someone had flipped a switch, his hands tightened and his hips charged harder between her open legs. She tilted her hips up to receive him, fast but steady. She ran her fingers over his soft hair, caressing his neck and the muscles of his broad shoulders.

"Feel good, sweetheart?" he whispered.

"Mmm. Yes." She pressed open-mouthed kisses to his cheek and jaw.

Cameron lifted one of her legs over his arm and lunged to the hilt. An involuntary cry left Simone's throat. Her toes curled into tight knots and she bit down on her lip, fingernails sinking into his back muscles as she fought to prolong the pleasurable tension.

Her determination was no match for his skill. He felt too good. Rotating his hips in a passion-filled rhythm, he sent her into orgasmic bliss where stars exploded behind her closed lids in a kaleidoscope of color. His mouth moved along her throat, adding another layer of sensation, and wails of pleasure emitted from her throat as he continued to thrust, panting, his tight body pounding, pounding, pounding into hers.

Until finally he could no longer hold out. A guttural groan shot from his chest and he surrendered to the passion. His entire body went tense before he let out a heavy breath and spent, he collapsed on top of her.

****

Something hard pushed against Simone's bottom. Her eyes fluttered open and she frowned, looking around at the unfamiliar surroundings. The room was dark, but slices of light slipped past the outer edge of the lowered Roman shades.

"You up?" Cameron's scratchy voice came from behind her, and then she recognized that the prodding came from the boner he had pushed up against her butt cheek.

One hand cupped her breast and squeezed. She moaned and arched her back, her nipple immediately hardening into the soft caress.

"What time is it?"

"Don't know. You have somewhere to be?"

He kissed her back, and she almost succumbed to the delicious sensation of his mouth on her skin. Fighting the urge, she rolled away and shoved her rumpled hair from her face. She searched for a clock, but there was none to be found on the bedside table.

"I need to know the time," Simone said.

"By the slant of light coming in, I'd say it's eightish."

"What!" Simone bolted from the bed.

Cameron sat up. "Where are you going?"

"I have an appointment at nine." She hurriedly dressed, pulling up her underwear, putting on her bra, and then wiggling to get the dress over her head. "I can't believe this," she muttered.

"Hey, slow down." He moved more slowly, rolling out of bed and tugging on his pants. "Do you want some coffee, or—"

"No, I can't. I have to go." Simone searched the room. Her eyes jerked back and forth in panic. "Where's my purse?"

"Downstairs."

"Oh, right." She hustled to the sliding translucent door that closed off the bedroom.

"Wait." Cameron grabbed her arm, frowning. "You're just going to leave?"

"I'm sorry, I have to go. I have an appointment in an hour, and I need to call my driver and have him get over here fast so I can get back to my condo, shower, change…" The enormity of everything she had to do overwhelmed her, and she pressed a hand to her forehead. She'd never get through in time. "I need to call my assistant so she can postpone my appointment. That's what I should do," she said, talking to herself.

How could she have allowed herself to get into this predicament? She slid the door open. Hurrying down the stairs, she squinted into the sunlight bursting through the long windows.

She snatched up her purse and looked up at Cameron, who paused halfway down the stairs. She took a moment to simply take him in. Barefoot and wearing only a pair of slacks, she was reminded again of her first impression of him—that of a god. What a body. He was covered in muscles, from his broad shoulders to his perfectly formed chest and flat stomach.

Simone hesitated. Maybe she could put off the appointment and stay longer. Just one more hour to bask in the heat of his touch and kisses.

No.

She had responsibilities. Sick children were depending on her.

"I'm sorry I have to run off like this."

Cameron shrugged. "No problem. Maybe we could hook up again some time."

She nodded. "I'd like that."

"I'll call you."

"Okay. And um…thanks for a nice night." She bit the inside of her lip. Was that an appropriate way to characterize their night together? *Nice?* Explosive or orgasmic would be a better adjective.

"You're welcome," he said, his mouth a full smile spreading to each corner of his face.

God, that smile. Would she ever see those beautiful lips and pretty white teeth again?

Simone lingered for a moment longer. She needed to leave but wondered if he really would call. She hoped so.

"Bye, Cameron."

Even if he didn't, she would be fine. She'd had a great time, and anyway, he wasn't Mr. Forever. He was just fun. That's what she'd told her sister.

She rushed out of the loft and was halfway down the hall when a smile spread across her face. She'd never before spent the night at a man's house the first night she went out with him, but she didn't regret it.

Not one bit.

Chapter Eight

Cameron and his siblings occasionally ate dinner together, and whenever they did, they ate at his place. Tonight was one of those nights.

He'd grilled two large butter-basted rib-eyes currently resting on the cutting board, and prepared a sauce béarnaise to be served over them. Oven-roasted asparagus was already on a white serving plate, and he was taking the Parmesan and herb-roasted potatoes out of the oven at the moment.

As he set the dishes on the steel table that seated eight on the other side of the kitchen pass-through, the front door opened and closed.

"Smells good in here." His brother Mason entered, wearing jeans and rubbing his stomach in preparation for the meal.

"I just finished. Where's Harp?" Cameron scraped the potatoes onto a serving dish and garnished them with chopped parsley.

"On her way, last time I talked to her." Scouring the selection of food, Mason licked his lips. "This looks good. I think you outdid yourself this time."

Cameron chuckled. "You say that every time." He didn't know if his meals were really that good, or if Mason graded on a curve because he didn't know how to cook. "Dad called, doing the usual check-in."

Their parents were traveling the country in a Winnebago, acting like tourists and visiting all the places they couldn't when they were a working couple raising a family.

"Where are they now?"

"San Diego. They're going to take a cruise to Mexico from there, and when they get back, head up the west coast to Seattle."

"I'm here!" Harper came into view in a pink sheath dress, her high heels sounding on the walnut wood floors. She dropped her purse on the dining room table. "I'm starved. Tell me you're finished."

"I'm finished. I know better than to keep the two of you waiting."

Although they were triplets, they didn't look much alike or act alike. Harper was the "baby," a bundle of energy with a toffee complexion and tiny like their mother. Having a beautiful sister meant Cameron and Mason were always in protective mode, which annoyed her.

Mason had the same dark complexion as Cameron but was an inch shorter. And while Cameron was proud of his physique built from years of outdoor activity, as a former Marine, his brother's body was a machine honed in missions around the world.

Mason invested in Club Masquerade from the outset but only recently returned to Atlanta after an explosion in Afghanistan left him wounded and one of his fellow Marines dead. Since his return home, he'd taken over the club's security. At times he favored his injured hand, and Cameron sometimes wondered how much pain he still suffered from. But Mason didn't talk much. He'd only share when ready.

They sat at the table, where the food had been set out family style, and passed the dishes around, filling their plates with heaping servings of the asparagus, potatoes, and sliced steak.

At first, the conversation turned to business, and Cameron gave them an update on a shooting that took place outside a club a couple of months ago. Two men had been killed, and the city council had pressured the liquor control board to temporarily suspend the club's liquor license. With no alcoholic beverages being served, business plummeted, forcing the owners to close the club.

"The good news is, those people are going to be looking for a place to party," Cameron said. "The bad news is, that could easily happen to us. We have to be diligent about security and make sure it doesn't."

Harper swirled a glass of pineapple and hibiscus cocktail. "I still think they overreacted. The incident took place outside the club," she said.

"You know as well as I do, that doesn't matter. They're always looking for a reason to shut us down, even though we pay a fortune in taxes." Cameron turned his attention to Mason. "We have to make sure we disperse the crowds and keep them from loitering around the club after they leave."

"My guys know what to do, but I'll brief them in our next meeting."

Harper set her glass on the table. "So what's this about you dating one of my clients?" she asked.

Cameron paused in the middle of slicing into his steak. "What are you talking about?"

"Don't act like you don't know what I'm talking about. Mason told me about how the super-rich socialite, Simone Brooks, threw up all over you. If she's not a billionaire, she's pretty darn close. Why'd you go out with her anyway? She doesn't seem like your type."

Harper was right. Simone wasn't his type. She appeared to be high-maintenance and certainly had the arrogance down, the way she pranced through Cooks Gadget Warehouse like she owned the place, with her red-bottomed shoes and Fendi purse. Still, he sensed a depth to her, hidden beneath the surface.

"She didn't throw up *all* over me. Mostly on my shoes." He shrugged. "And why wouldn't I go out with her? She's a woman." Cameron ate a piece of ribeye.

He'd never made a secret of his appreciation of the opposite sex. He loved everything about women, from their soft curves to their saucy smiles.

"What happened when you went out?" Harper asked.

"Had a good time." He smiled.

Harper rolled her eyes. "Ugh. You didn't."

"I can't help it if I'm irresistible."

Mason chuckled and shook his head. "Do you ever turn down a piece of ass?"

"Do you?"

Mason dated, but Cameron suspected he carried a torch for their childhood friend, London, though he'd never admitted it. Harper had been trying to get the two of them together for years.

She waved a hand in front of Cameron's face to bring his attention back to her. "So what's the deal? Are you two dating?"

"We hooked up. We may hook up again, that's all. I called her the other day to see if she wanted to get together, but she's in London and doesn't know when she'll be back."

He'd been a bit disappointed to learn Simone was out of the country and surprised she hadn't said a word to him about the trip. The day after their night together, she'd rushed out without even having breakfast. It burned to have her dash from his bed so early in the morning and leave him behind. He'd felt...*used*.

"At least she doesn't have your nose wide open like the other one," Mason said.

"Hey, she didn't have my nose wide open, but I did screw up by sleeping with one of the owners of the company. Hell hath no fury like a woman scorned."

When the short-lived affair ended, so did his position as general manager of the restaurant.

Harper tapped a nail on the metal table. "Hmm. Does Simone have a job? I mean, what does she *do*, exactly?"

"Charity work. That's all I know." Cameron still didn't have a full grasp on Simone's role at the foundation. Essentially, she sounded like a professional volunteer. "I have plans with Sherry Stone anyway," Cameron said.

"The business banker?" Mason asked.

"That's the one."

"I guess your persistence paid off," Harper said drily.

"You could say that." Cameron chuckled softly. Sherry had turned him down several times when he asked her out, even though she eye-fucked him every time she saw him at the bank. They'd played a little cat and mouse game for months. Flirt. Laugh. Say goodbye. Start again the next time he went into the branch.

Harper shook her head in disgust. "How do you keep up with all these different women?"

"Skill and practice." He stopped teasing long enough to look at his sister with concern. "If you'd stop working so hard, you'd have time to meet someone yourself. I keep telling you to give your staff more control."

"It's hard letting go. I know how important it is to give the celebrity clients extra attention, and to be honest, I feel as if I'm best suited to make sure everything runs smoothly." She shrugged. "But I promise to take your suggestion under consideration. How's that?"

"Let the right man come along and she'll gladly change her tune," Mason said.

"Enough about my lack of love life, you two. By the way, this ribeye is delicious."

"Subtle. Real subtle, Harp," Cameron said.

She wrinkled her nose at him and they had a good laugh.

At the end of the meal, Cameron brought out a simple dessert—a tray of ice cream sandwiches made of strawberry ice cream and ginger cookies.

Harper's eyes went wide. "No. You. Didn't."

"Yes. I. Did."

"Shit, I haven't had one of these in years," Mason said, plucking one from the tray. "Dad used to make these all the time."

Cameron nodded. "Made the ice cream from scratch, too, remember? He used that old hand crank machine."

"It made the best ice cream, though." Harper took a bite and closed her eyes. "Mmm. This brings back so many memories."

"Sitting on the back porch, eating ice cream sandwiches after Sunday dinner," Mason said. He took another bite.

"It's not the back porch, but I have a terrace," Cameron suggested.

"Let's do it." Harper jumped up first.

The three of them went out onto the terrace and ate the ice cream and cookie dessert, watching the sun go down, with the noise of the street below. The perfect end to the meal.

And everything Cameron had said to Harper and Mason about Simone...well, he almost believed it.

Chapter Nine

Once a month, Sylvie Johnson insisted on having lunch with her children. When Simone had lived in Seattle, she had missed the lunch dates with her family and sometimes flew back and spent the day so she could experience that closeness. The monthly meals were not only for their mother's benefit, but a way for them all to catch up and maintain their familial bond.

Having returned earlier than expected from London, Simone spent the last couple of days catching up on foundation business. Today she joined Ella in their mother's plush office, an expansive domain decorated in tan and gold and splashes of pale rose, while they waited for Reese and Stephan to arrive.

Sylvie sat behind her desk in a plush ivory chair from her high-end line of office furniture designed with the female executive in mind. As a young woman she'd had no interest in the family's beer and restaurant empire, and had used her inheritance to build businesses that she had an interest in. For her that meant furniture, film and television projects, and anything related to the fashion industry. Her line of clothing and makeup products were made with only the finest materials sourced from all over the world and sold in exclusive stores. The Sylvie brand, popular among the rich and famous, was synonymous with extravagance and quality.

On the filmmaking front, she'd produced a number of independent films that turned into huge moneymakers and financed a few documentaries. The paperwork she was going over was for an almost concluded contest where documentary filmmakers submitted proposals for funding. Her committee whittled down thousands of entrants to twenty-five. She and a core group of the committee would then decide which of the twenty-five her company would invest in.

"Did Simone mention to you that she cooked dinner last night? By herself?" Across the room, Ella smiled. She thought it was funny Simone had been spending so much time cooking.

The truth was, she'd been practicing so when she saw Cameron again, she could impress him with her improved culinary skills.

The midday sun came through the sheer curtains on the window at Sylvie's back. Looking up from the paperwork in front of her, she said, "Cooked? You could have ordered something to eat, surely? Is Martha ill?"

"She's not ill. I just wanted to," Simone answered, rather proud of herself.

Before the trip to London, she'd worked in the kitchen a few times with Martha, but this time she'd wanted to handle the meal all alone. She gave Martha a list of ingredients to purchase at the store and prepared the entire meal herself by carefully following the recipe instructions.

Martha had teasingly said that she would soon have to look for a new job. They'd laughed at that, knowing no such thing was about to happen. As much as she enjoyed her new hobby of cooking, Simone knew she could not run her household without Martha.

"You wanted to what, darling?" Sylvie asked.

"Cook," Simone answered.

Her mother's brow furrowed in confusion. "You *wanted* to cook? This is a very confusing conversation." Sylvie removed her designer glasses and placed them on the desktop.

"It's fun and something different to do. I like being able to make a meal for myself." Simone took a deep breath, ready to share her experience with Cameron. "A couple of weeks ago, I went out with a man, and he took me on a date to a school where we cooked dinner and then ate what we'd made. Ever since then, I've been practicing and Martha's been helping me. Last night I made roasted chicken with brown rice and steamed vegetables."

Pause.

"Darling, are you all right?" Genuine concern filled Sylvie's eyes.

"I'm fine."

"Then why are you *cooking*? Like a servant? And who is this man who put you to work on a *date*, for heaven's sake? That sounds absolutely horrid."

The conversation quickly tumbled downhill.

Realizing her teasing had created an uncomfortable situation for Simone, Ella jumped into the conversation. "Mother, we've cooked before. We used to make you breakfast, remember?"

Sylvie smiled then, a beatific expression as she reflected on the past. "Yes, I recall those cute little heart-shaped pancakes with scrambled eggs and fruit you all made for me as children. And all of you would come into the bedroom with flowers to wish me a happy Mother's Day. Those were wonderful times." Wistfulness filled her voice at the memories. "But an entire dinner seems rather extreme."

"Simone was just having fun." Ella caught Simone's eye and smiled, her expression at once soothing and apologetic.

"Well I certainly hope it was fun," Sylvie said. She twisted her attention back to Simone. "I didn't even know you were dating. Who is this young man? Do I know him?"

Simone didn't know how to answer that question, and she took too long formulating an answer. Sylvie lifted her eyebrows impatiently.

"You don't know him," Simone replied.

"May I have a name?"

Simone smoothed the full skirt of her dress. "His name is Cameron Bennett. He owns Club Masquerade."

Sylvie gasped and clutched her pearls. "Is that some kind of swinging club?"

Ella snickered, and Simone darted a glare in her direction, which promptly shut her up.

"It's a nightclub. The hottest one in Atlanta," Simone answered, oddly proud. "It's an upscale place that hosts celebrity parties, and they have different events like Wind Down Wednesday and stuff like that. I threw Kim's divorce party there."

Sylvie folded her hands atop the contracts and took a good look at her daughter, disapproval etched in the fine lines around her mouth. "I realize good men are hard to find, but a nightclub owner? I certainly hope your little dalliance doesn't distract you from your work at the foundation."

She didn't say it, but the word *again* was understood in the scolding.

"I won't let it." Embarrassment and guilt burned Simone's cheeks.

"I'm not saying this to be cruel, but you said you wanted to get married. Do you recall what happened in Seattle?"

The fiasco in Seattle had been the biggest mistake she'd ever made. Jack was an administrator for a cancer research facility the Johnson Foundation partially funded. He turned out to be an ass.

True enough they'd had their differences, and after breaking up, he set about to systematically tarnish her good name. He attacked not only her, but the foundation's credibility. He accused her of being pushy, entitled, and arrogant and implied the funds the foundation raised did not go toward the programs as reported. He pointed out that Simone often traveled first class or by private jet, and that while she wasn't on the payroll, it was questionable she needed all the perks that she was allotted, completely ignoring the tens of millions she helped raise and the huge sums donated to the cancer facility. He eventually lost his position, as they could not afford to alienate the Johnson Foundation and lose the money donated every year.

"Keep in mind that the differences between you and someone who does not have our type of money sounds nice and is exciting at first, but men are simply incapable of handling strong women like us."

Here it comes.

"Look at your father. Our relationship didn't last, did it? He's gone. Ella's husband. Gone."

Across the room, Ella stiffened.

"The situation with Jack was certainly not your fault," her mother continued. When she was on a roll, she didn't know when to stop. "But once again he was not accustomed to our level of wealth, and because of that he made gross accusations that tarnished the good name of the foundation, and you as well. My darling, you're not getting any younger. Why put yourself through that again? Why waste your time with a man who you know you won't marry, when there are so many eligible young men available. In fact…" Sylvie flipped open her royal blue planner and tapped a page with a cream painted fingernail. "I have lunch tomorrow with Agnes Duvalier. I don't have to tell you that the Duvaliers have amassed a huge real estate fortune and she's interested in expanding her investments with some money left to her by an aunt, who recently passed away. I'll probably have her invest in a small independent film first. Anyway, I said all that to say her son, Albert, is in town with her, and he's single." She used the French pronunciation of his name—*Al-bear*. "And..." her voice dropped to a conspiratorial level and excitement sparked in her eyes. "...he's looking for a wife. Absolutely, positively, ready to settle down from what I understand. I can arrange a meeting within the next few days. What do you think?"

Simone thought getting set up was a terrible idea, because she was not interested in Albert. She hadn't seen him in several years. However, her mother did have a point about the differences between her and Cameron, and there was no reason why she couldn't at least give Albert a shot. She'd simply postpone setting up another date with Cameron until she wrapped up the meeting with Albert.

"Sounds great," she said.

Ella pursed her lips thoughtfully but remained silent.

"Perfect." Sylvie wrote a note in her planner. "Now, where are your brothers?"

Asking the question seemed to have the effect of conjuring them. Stephan and Reese traipsed in with huge grins, looking exactly like what they were—rich playboys without a care in the world.

Sylvie did not smile back. "We have a reservation. You're late."

"Sorry, Mother. We got sidetracked." Stephan's light brown eyes, which matched their mother's, gleamed with mischief. No doubt whatever had sidetracked him had two X chromosomes.

"We'll pay for lunch to make it up to you," Reese offered, the more serious of the two.

"Yes, you will." Sylvie rose from the chair. "Let's go. We're already late, and I'm quite hungry."

Their mother walked ahead in a black pantsuit from the Sylvie clothing line and they followed behind. On the elevator ride down, Simone barely heard the conversation taking place around her.

All she could think about was Cameron and the next time she'd have a chance to see him.

Chapter Ten

Cameron had gone in early to meet with staff and make sure they could handle the night without him. He almost felt guilty about taking Saturday night off, he hadn't done it in so long, but intended to enjoy himself. Especially since a peculiar sense of unease stayed with him all day. He was tense and restless. Had been for weeks. He simply couldn't relax and looked forward to dinner and later sinking his body into the lovely woman at his side.

He parked his SUV and walked around to the passenger side of the vehicle. Nearby, the Chattahoochee River sparkled under the artificial lights, rolling past the landscaped grounds of Kayak, an upscale restaurant tucked away behind one of the city's most exclusive neighborhoods. The late meal was the perfect end to an evening that started with a one-hour jazz performance at a small venue nearby.

Cameron opened the door for Sherry. Their date couldn't have come at a better time. He needed a distraction from thoughts of Simone. He hadn't seen her in three weeks, yet every time he walked into his loft, he swore he smelled remnants of her perfume.

He helped Sherry down from the vehicle. She was an attractive woman, with golden yellow skin and reddish blond curls that formed a halo around her head. She had a banging body, the kind that looked amazing in tight and short dresses, exactly like the coral mini exposing the shapely length of her legs. Anticipation buzzed through his blood. He fully expected to end the evening in her bed.

"You haven't said anything about my dress," Sherry said, smoothing her hands over her hips.

"I didn't know I had to. I thought the way my tongue was hanging out of my head made it clear what I thought."

He should have paid her a compliment right away. Especially since it was obvious she'd gone to so much trouble to impress him. She giggled and slapped his chest. "Cam, you're a mess."

They walked arm in arm into Kayak and through the small foyer toward the host stand.

Inside, Cameron's gaze landed on a couple in front of them. The hairs on the back of his neck stood on end, and his feet stopped moving. Simone stood there with a light-skinned brother. Tall and with curly hair, he looked distinguished with modern square spectacles and a couple of days' growth of facial hair. She hung on his arm much the same way Sherry hung on Cameron's.

"Is something wrong?" Sherry asked. Her gaze traveled in the same direction as his.

"No," Cameron said shortly.

They resumed walking and upon approach, Simone looked up, and when she saw them, her eyes widened.

"Simone," Cameron said.

Unable to help himself, his gaze dragged down her body, admiring the way the loose skirt of the strapless dress managed to show her curves. The tight bodice stretched over full breasts, and the slit at the front teased the eye with a hint of leg. It looked simple enough, but the dress probably cost the same as the average worker's weekly wages.

"What a coincidence," Cameron continued.

Simone's brown eyes flicked over Sherry, but her face betrayed no emotion. Only a fractional tightening of her lips before she smiled pleasantly. "Hello. Albert Duvalier, this is Cameron Bennett, a friend."

He involuntarily stiffened. For some reason, the lukewarm description pissed him off. Friend? A friend who'd had her bent over the foot of the bed while she moaned his name into the mattress.

Cameron extended his hand to the other man. "Now, now, we were more than friends," he said, taking Albert's hand and giving it two hard pumps. Jeez, he was acting like an ass but couldn't help himself.

Simone's eyes widened, and Albert frowned, dropping an arm across Simone's shoulder. Cameron watched the move with a clenched jaw and tightened his grip on his date's hand.

Sherry cleared her throat beside him.

"Where are my manners? Sherry Stone, this is Simone Brooks. Back from London, I see."

"Nice to meet you." Simone smiled again. Serene. Calm. While the fire of jealousy raged within him.

"Likewise." Sherry stepped closer to Cameron, making sure their sides were flush against each other.

"You have a reservation?" the male host asked.

Cameron had been so busy with his obsession with Simone, he hadn't even checked in. "Yes." He gave his name and the man confirmed the reservation. Minutes later, a different host escorted Simone and Albert to their table, and a hostess led Cameron and his date back to theirs.

Luckily—or unluckily—they were placed near each other, which gave Cameron an ideal view of the grounds with the river beyond, and a good view of the back of Albert's head.

"Is everything okay?" Sherry asked quietly, glancing up from the menu.

The oddly tight smile on her lips shook Cameron from his haze.

Hell, what was he doing? Here he sat with a beautiful, willing woman and all he could think about was the liar two tables away. In London, my ass. She'd blown him off to make plans with this Duvalier dude.

"Everything's great." His smile was meant to appease and smooth her concerns, which seemed to do the trick, because she tossed a saucy smile his way, her eyes filled with heat and a promise of good things to come.

The second she returned her attention to the options on the menu, Cameron's gaze drifted to Simone's table. Her bigheaded date shifted and blocked his view of her face, and he grunted his discontent, quickly covering the noise by clearing his throat.

"Have you eaten here before?" Sherry asked.

"A few times," Cameron answered, glancing up at Albert's head again.

Every ten seconds his eyes found their way back to the other table. He continued like that for several minutes, interrupted only when the waiter came by to tell them the special and take their drink orders. Occasionally, Albert moved to the side or leaned forward, and Cameron caught a glimpse of Simone's face. He kept his eyes on her during those periods, even though he knew he shouldn't.

She offered her broad smile to the other man, which lit up her face and eyes. It irritated the hell out of Cameron that this man was the recipient of the full magnitude of her lips and dimples.

With a start, he realized Sherry was talking to him, and he hadn't heard a thing she'd said. He tugged on his black tie. "What did you say?"

"I said, I haven't had fish in a while. I was thinking about getting the swordfish. It sounds delicious." Keeping her eyes downcast, she traced a nail along the words on the menu.

Simone laughed out loud. A sexy, alluring sound that drifted on the air to his table. Then she rested her chin on her hand and gazed at Albert, her eyes soft, her lips tilted into a welcoming curve.

Anger burned inside Cameron. Was she doing that shit on purpose?

"You can't go wrong with anything you choose," he said absentmindedly.

The waiter came by, a happy-looking guy smiling so hard he could have swallowed his ears. "Have you decided?" he asked.

"I have." Sherry looked expectantly across the table.

Cameron had barely paid attention to the choices on the menu since he sat down. "I need a little more time," he mumbled. The waiter promised to return in a few minutes and disappeared. Cameron glanced at the entrees and chose the duck, something he hadn't had in a long time, and set the menu aside.

He sipped from the glass of water in front of him.

"Thank you for inviting me out tonight." Sherry reached across the table and enclosed one of his hands in both of hers.

"Thank you for accepting."

"You're welcome."

She really was a good-looking woman, with full lips painted an eye-catching shade of red that ordinarily would have him thinking lewd thoughts. Instead, all he could think about was the shade of red on Simone's lips.

He took another sip of water, set the glass on the table, and then picked it back up and swallowed half of the contents. He was burning up.

"So…tonight…" Sherry let the words trail off suggestively and stroked a nail along the back of his hand.

He made himself think of those long nails dragging down his back. He imagined her as a wildcat in bed.

"I have a little surprise for you," Sherry continued. She looked up at him between her lashes.

"You do, huh?" *Concentrate. You'll get laid tonight if you don't screw this up.*

"Mmm-hmm. I've had my eye on you for a while."

As if he didn't know. Sherry wasn't exactly known for her subtlety, but she'd certainly made him wait long enough. "Oh really?"

"Mmm-hmm. Ever since the first day I saw you signing documents with my colleague."

"Well, I've had my eye on you, too, and I'm glad I didn't give up."

"I'm glad you didn't, either."

Simone got up from her chair, and before he had time to think about what he was doing, Cameron shot up from his. The action was automatic.

Sherry's mouth fell open. "What—"

"I'll be right back."

He didn't know where Simone was headed. Bathroom, probably. If that was the case, so was he. He followed her through the crowded dining room and past the bar. When they entered the back hallway, she swung around.

"What do you want, Cam?"

What did he want? He was like a man possessed. "Is that your boyfriend?" The words came out before he could stop them.

Simone tossed her glossy hair and glared at him. "Jealous?"

"Hardly."

She crossed her arms over her chest. "Then don't worry about it."

"I'm not." He stepped closer. A mistake, of course, because the scent of her perfume filled his nostrils—the same earthy fragrance that haunted the loft—and heated his blood. "I'm curious about what you're doing. Three weeks ago you were in my apartment, making love to me like a woman possessed, and now you're with this guy?"

Her eyes went icy. "You have some nerve. Is that your girlfriend?"

"I don't have to answer to you," he said.

"And I don't have to answer to you," she snapped. "Whatever she is, stop ignoring her. It's rude."

She tossed her hair, the movement making the glossy strands ripple and elongating her neck in a tempting way. If she did that again, he was going to grab her by the hair.

"You're right. I shouldn't ignore Sherry. A sexy woman like that deserves my undivided attention."

Her lips tightened. "Exactly. I certainly plan to give Albert my undivided attention tonight. I haven't had sex in a few weeks, so I'm a bit overdue and feeling kind of horny. If you'll excuse me…"

Cameron froze as Simone sauntered off with her trademark walk, hips swinging from side to side in a hypnotizing fashion.

Three weeks. Three long, barren weeks since he'd sipped the nectar of her kisses and felt her soft skin under his hands. And she was taunting him with another man.

Rage exploded inside him. With three long strides, he overtook the distance between them. His hand snapped to her wrist, closing over the delicate bones with force and yanking her around to face him.

She gasped, her startled gaze landing on his face. Fine brows descended over widened eyes.

The next thing Cameron knew, his legs were eating up the carpet as he pulled Simone along behind him.

Chapter Eleven

Simone glanced over her shoulder, but neither Albert nor Sherry could see them from this angle. Good thing, too, because Cameron obviously didn't care if their dates or anyone else observed them together.

He pushed her ahead of him through a door, and she stumbled into an opulent bathroom, bright lights glaring overhead and bouncing off the Italian tile and expensive fixtures.

Simone placed her hands on her hips and tilted her nose toward the ceiling. "How dare you manhandle me?"

With a cursory glance, Cameron made sure the two stalls were empty and then snapped his gaze back to her, taking slow, measured steps to back her up until she hit the cold wall.

"You didn't mind when I manhandled you at the loft," he said softly.

Then she went there—to the memory of him sliding the cheeky down her hips and fisting a hand in her hair as she straddled him. She recalled the hunger in his voice when he whispered in her ear all the delicious things he planned to do her. His voice raw. The words dirty. His hands rough as he lifted her into his thrusting hips.

"Different time, different place."

"Why aren't you in London?"

"I came back early."

"You didn't call."

She did, but she'd never give him the satisfaction of knowing that. She'd called the club and they'd told her that he wasn't working tonight, and when she called his home she didn't receive an answer. She'd wanted to make plans for when Albert left town tomorrow. But here he was, not thinking about her nearly as much as she was thinking about him. Certainly not with the hot woman seated at his table outside, wearing what could only be described as a fuck-me dress.

"I didn't know I was supposed to call."

"I guess not. You didn't call to tell me you were going to leave. You didn't call to tell me you were back."

Did she hear resentment in his voice?

Then he was right there, in front her, pressing his palm to the wall above her head.

"You planning to sleep with him tonight?" Cameron asked, his voice sounding strangled.

"Stop it, Cam." She wanted to touch him. She ached for the contact. Instead, her fingers clutched the soft material of her dress.

Then she saw the way his eyes lowered to her lips and his nostrils flared.

"Cam…" She didn't know why she said his name like that, in such a pleading way. She only knew she needed him and suspected he needed her, too.

"Let me give you something to think about while you're with him."

Before he even moved, she guessed his intent. She wanted the kiss, maybe even more than he did. She hadn't stopped thinking about him since she left his bed.

Cameron's fingers slid under her hair to the back of her neck and he leaned in, tugging her forward at the same time so that she was anchored to his body before his head dipped down to hers.

Impact.

A sweet explosion at the collision of mouth to mouth.

Right away, a current of energy cycled through Simone's body. The soft lips covering hers opened and closed in a domineering caress. Her hands slid around his neck, drawing him closer as she lifted onto the tips of her shoes and strained against him.

Cameron's kissing game was on point. He didn't simply raise the bar. He demolished it with a bat and splintered it into little pieces. Plucking her lower lip between his, he sucked, then dived in for more with his tongue.

The kiss deepened into a greedy, open-mouthed attack, turning harder and more intense. Their breaths commingled. Their moans slipped over each other, making it unclear where one ended and the other began.

One hand eased up and down her spine, then ran up under the hem of her dress and gripped her behind. Simone shivered, her nipples pebbling against his hard chest. Cameron kissed her neck, groaning and releasing heavy puffs of air from his nose and mouth.

"Taste so good, sweetheart," he groaned.

Her own breathing pattern changed, turning into a jagged, irregular sound as his hands and mouth thrilled every inch of skin they touched.

His fingers dallied around her hips, tracing the line of her underwear. Simone let out a tiny little whimper and closed her eyes, her belly trembling in anticipation of his touch.

"You're driving me insane," he muttered against the side of her mouth.

When his finger slid beneath the edge of her panties, she gasped and fisted her hands behind his head.

A rough swear dragged from his vocal chords as he shoved two fingers into the moist cleft between her thighs.

"Cam…" This time his name came out as a raw, unfiltered moan.

Clutching him close, Simone eased her legs wider so he could do as he pleased. His fingers glided in and out, stroking the wet inner muscles of her sex. She wanted to beg. She wanted to plead with him not to stop as she rubbed her cheek against his strong jaw. She turned her face into his neck, sucking on his Adam's apple and kissing his neck and the line of his jaw.

Goodness, he smelled so good. The spicy aroma of his cologne was at once familiar and intoxicating. It had lingered in her skin after she left his bed and tortured her on the ride back to her condo. Only through a long, steamy shower did she finally manage to rid herself of the scent of him.

With his fingers between her legs and his soft lips sucking on her neck, her body tightened with a pending climax. She held him even closer, lifting her aching bosom toward his mouth.

He teased her with soft kisses over the crests of her breasts and dragged his tongue over the line of her cleavage, leaving a moist trail across her skin. Simone's head tipped back to the wall and she strained closer still, angling her lower body toward him, all the while maintaining an open-legged stance as he worked those long fingers over the swollen clit between her thighs.

Someone could bust in on them at any minute, but that logical thought disappeared with all others when the tightening in her abdomen released, and ecstasy exploded and surged through her loins. Her knees buckled and she fell back against the wall to stay upright. Trembling, she cried out, and immediately his lips came crashing down on hers to muffle the sound.

The kiss only lasted a few seconds, and when he released her mouth, Simone followed. It wasn't enough that the stroke of his long fingers had brought her to orgasm. She clung to him, seeking more intimacy. Seeking affection.

He pressed his face into her neck as Simone fought to bring her breathing under control.

"Cam." She kissed his ear and jaw.

Slowly, he lifted his head and they made eye contact. "Consider that my gift to you. The best orgasm you'll have all night."

She felt bereft when he eased his hand from between her thighs, leaning against the wall for support since her weak and wobbly legs were practically useless.

Cameron cursed, a loud f-bomb that echoed in the room. Simone winced at the angry sound and watched as he went over to the sink and washed his hands, rubbing them clean of any evidence of what they'd done. Not once did he look at himself in the mirror, as if he couldn't stand the sight of his own face.

He braced his hands on the edge of the sink. "This is my fault," he murmured. "I came after you, but I'll leave you alone so you can go back to Mr. Duvalier."

Cameron walked out, his gait stiff but forceful. Not once did he look at her again.

Simone pounded the wall behind her with angry fists. How humiliating that she'd allowed him to bring her to orgasm with just the stroke of his fingers, while their dates sat out in the dining room waiting for them.

She didn't know who made her angrier. Him, or herself.

****

Cameron sat down and smiled across the table at Sherry. Thank goodness his suit jacket hid the erection he couldn't squash.

"Sorry about that. I had to...take care of something."

Her gaze flickered over him. "Did you?" An eyebrow raised in inquiry, her expression cool.

58

"Yeah. Nothing important." Cameron shifted in the chair and rubbed his hands down his thighs, body humming. He needed a strong drink. Fast.

Sherry extended a white cloth napkin to him.

Cameron frowned. Taking it, he asked, "What's this for?"

"There's lipstick on your collar. And on your mouth."

She shot knives at him with her piercing gaze. Folding her arms over her chest, her attention turned to the nighttime landscape outside the window.

The heat of shame burned across Cameron's neck and chest. He hadn't checked the mirror in the bathroom before he left. "Sherry, I—"

Another angry glance flew across the table before she swung her head to stare out the window again. "Take me home."

He was horny as hell and couldn't get laid. His night was ruined.

Cameron swiped his mouth and faint red color transferred to the napkin. There was nothing he could say to make it up to Sherry. He was truly an ass.

Simone came back into the dining room, her hips swinging with each graceful movement of her legs. Their gazes briefly met before she sat down.

He watched as she reapplied her lipstick, smoothing the stick over her full mouth and then rubbing her lips together—the way women do—to evenly distribute the color.

Scorching heat filled his chest. The heat of want. The heat of desire. The heat of deprivation.

Simone rested her chin in her hand and smiled across the table at Albert. Completely entranced, all Cameron could think was that he should be the one sitting across from her.

And that he wanted that smile for himself.

Chapter Twelve

Cameron pulled up to the front door of the nightclub. Having already called ahead, a wiry attendant named Rob, wearing a friendly smile and the standard black slacks, white shirt, and lavender bow tie, greeted him as he descended from the vehicle.

"Good afternoon, Cameron," the young man said.

Cameron tossed him the key. "Be careful with my baby," he warned.

"Always." Rob hopped into the vehicle with a little too much enthusiasm, and drove away toward the employee parking area.

Strolling into the dim club, Cameron surveyed the interior. Later, the place would be bouncing and alive with energy, but at five o'clock in the afternoon was much more low-key. Bartenders stocked the spirits at the circular bar in the middle of the floor in preparation for the Wind Down Wednesday crowd, and a few of the waitresses chatted in a corner. The combination of black leotards overlaid with lace, heels, fishnet stockings, and lavender bowties was eye-catching.

"Hello ladies," he greeted them on his way to the elevator.

"Hey, Cameron," they sang, doing flutter waves and giving him seductive smiles—the same ones they bestowed on clients who gave them additional gratuity above and beyond what was built into the bills.

Cameron took the elevator to the top floor and immediately went to work, running through revenue from the previous night, and returning a few phone calls. He took care of a dispute with a vendor and paid some bills electronically. He then did his usual walk through of the club before the late night crowd arrived—greeting patrons in the restaurant and checking in with the kitchen, and the managers, before heading back to his office on the third floor.

He bumped into Harper in management's private hallway, clutching her iPad, as usual. "Mason's looking for you," she said.

"Did he say why?" Cameron asked.

"He said he has something to show you on the monitors." She tilted her head to the side. "Are you okay? You look...I don't know, weird."

"Nah, I'm fine."

"You were frowning."

"Was I?"

She lifted a brow. "You're still thinking about her, aren't you?" she asked.

He couldn't get anything past his siblings. "Who, Simone? Hell, no," he lied, rolling his shoulders.

Harper crossed her arms. "Uh-huh."

"Don't you have a party to tend to?" Cameron asked, walking toward the stairwell.

"Nice way to change the subject." She headed in the opposite direction.

Cameron turned back to his sister. "Hey, Harp, let me know when you get a call from a Sandy Belkin. Put her in the White Room and make sure she gets the star treatment."

She placed a hand on her hips. "Don't I always take care of your groupies?"

"Ha. Ha. You're hilarious. She's not a groupie. I met her at the market today and gave her a VIP pass for her and guests. Told her to call you when she's ready to use it. She works at the radio station, so we could get some free publicity out of her visit."

Harper walked away and called over her shoulder, "Don't worry, I got you."

A few minutes later, Cameron pressed his thumb to the pad outside the security room. Inside, Mason and a team of four kept an eye on the interior and exterior of the club.

"You wanted to see me," Cameron said.

Mason waved him over. "There's something I need you to look at."

One of the security personnel left his chair so Cameron could sit and get a good look at the screen.

Mason zoomed the camera to a man standing against the wall, holding a beer. He wore a black button down and jeans and was staring across at the bar.

"That guy." Mason pointed. "He comes in here all the time and just stands against the wall, like he's doing now." He stuck one of the gourmet lollipops he often carried into his mouth.

"Who is he?"

"Don't know, but something about him rubs me the wrong way. He's not causing any problems. He just makes me uneasy."

"Should we have one of the bouncers approach him?"

Mason twirled the red candy in his mouth for a few seconds before answering. "I don't think he's an immediate threat," he said slowly. "Let me keep an eye on him a little bit longer."

"Okay." Cameron stood. He trusted his brother's instincts. "Keep me posted."

"I will."

Cameron went back to his office and buckled down to write a list of tasks that needed to be accomplished over the next few days. After almost an hour, he tossed the pen across the desk, removed his reading glasses, and reclined in the chair. With a lull in his workload, his mind returned again and again to Simone.

Did she sleep with that guy, Albert?

He stood abruptly from the chair and poured himself a glass of lukewarm water.

Fuck her.

He paced to the window and slowly drank the water. Night had fallen, and he stared out at the illuminated street below and cars crawling along between the buildings.

Why couldn't he stop thinking about her? They didn't have any hold on each other, and he could have his pick of almost any single woman who walked into the club tonight. Yet she was the one who stayed on his brain.

He set the empty glass on the sill and paced the floor of his office like a caged tiger.

Granted, the interlude in the bathroom should not have happened while they were both on dates with other people, but it didn't mean anything. *She* didn't mean anything to him.

He stopped pacing, eyes landing on the building across the street, where squares of light poured from the windows.

Sex with her had been mind-blowing, but so what? He'd had sex with plenty of women.

So why did she occupy his thoughts almost nonstop? All his senses reminded him of everything related to her—her scent on his fingers, the taste of her on his tongue. Last night, aroused to the point of discomfort, he'd used his hand to relieve himself, releasing a groan of simultaneous pleasure and longing because, despite the temporary relief, true satisfaction could only come from having her.

There was really only one solution to this problem.

Cameron snatched up the phone and dialed her number. The digits were burned into his brain even though he'd barely used them.

A female voice answered on the first ring.

"Hello?"

Probably her assistant, Adele.

"May I speak to Simone, please," he said.

"May I ask who's calling?" she said in a cautious voice.

"Cameron Bennett. I'm one of the owners of Club Masquerade, where you organized the divorce party. I need to speak to Simone. Is she available?"

"One moment."

The phone went silent when she muted the line, and Cameron waited anxiously for Simone, resuming his trek back and forth in the same line, probably wearing a hole in the carpet but unable to stop moving.

"Hello?"

The sound of her voice arrested his footsteps, and the amount of relief that flooded him not only shocked but angered him. That this woman could have so much control over his emotional state infuriated him.

"Do you have plans tonight?" He asked without ceremony.

A few seconds passed before she responded. "Why?"

"I want you to come to the loft."

"And why would I do that? What is this about?" she asked, her voice unnervingly cool and extra proper.

Her tone should have doused the flames of his desire. Instead, the sound of her voice simply inflamed him. The cool façade was merely a front, hiding the sensual creature she was underneath.

Heat clawed at his loins.

"You know what this is about. We have unfinished business."

The gentle noise of her breathing filled the line, and he could barely discern the quiet conversation of two other female voices talking to each other in the background.

He waited with a tight and heavy knot of lead in his belly.

"All right," she finally said.

The lead weight lessened. "Can you be there by midnight?"

"Yes, I can."

"This time, bring a bag. No running out at the crack of dawn."

"It wasn't the crack of dawn."

"I'll see you at twelve."

Cameron hung up and ran a hand down his face. He was probably out of his mind, but he needed Simone out of his system and out of his head. Maybe he could finally resolve the restlessness that constantly plagued him.

At least, that's what he hoped.

****

"What did he want?" Ella sat across from Simone in the limo, eyebrows drawn low over her eyes.

Simone handed the phone to her assistant seated beside her. "He wants me to come see him."

"And you're going to?" Ella asked, incredulous. Understandably so, since Simone had told her about the night at the restaurant and how he'd left her in the bathroom to go back to his date. She herself had ended the night with a chaste kiss to Albert's cheek, but she wondered if Cameron had slept with Sherry.

She didn't want to think about it and shifted on the seat as the car rolled down the highway on their way to dinner. "I have to see what he wants."

"You know what he wants."

Simone crossed her legs and stared out the window.

A juvenile could figure out what he wanted. The pressing problem was that she wanted it, too. His touch remained imprinted on her like a brand. She relived the night they spent together in vivid detail, craving more. Sex toys were inadequate. She only wanted Cameron.

"Simone, don't do this. It's a mistake."

"Is it?" She was tired of everyone telling her what to do and how to behave. "I'm an adult. I can make my own decisions."

"Cameron makes you lose control."

She fiddled with the gold bracelets on her wrists. "I can handle him," she said.

"Neither one of us believes that," Ella said.

Simone shrugged. "Doesn't matter. I'm willing to take the risk."

"He's going to hurt you. Disappoint you."

"It won't come to that."

Both sisters stared at each other before Ella let out a frustrated sigh of acceptance. "So you're canceling?"

"I have to go home and get ready."

"What am I supposed to tell our friends?"

They were meeting friends for drinks, but she couldn't possibly do that now. She needed to get home and take a shower, do her hair, refresh her makeup, and pack a bag.

"Tell them something came up."

"So you want me to lie?"

"It's not a lie, but if you want, you can give them the details. I don't care."

Ella folded her arms across her torso. "You know Mother would never approve of what you're doing, and there was a time you would never go against her wishes."

Simone glanced at her assistant, who tucked a lock of dark hair behind her ear and shifted uncomfortably as their voices rose. "You're not exactly the poster child for doing what Mother asks, either. You went against her wishes after you met your husband."

Their mother had mapped out their lives, making sure they attended the right parties and met the most eligible bachelors. At times, Simone had felt like a show dog, put on display for men to figuratively poke and prod as they determined whether or not she was wife material.

As far as Sylvie was concerned, Ella and Simone were too emotional—thinking with their hearts instead of their brains. A solid relationship decision meant a man of their ilk. Someone wealthy and who understood their way of life.

Simone tugged at her bracelets, watching as the jewelry sparkled beneath the passing lights. "Maybe I want to do what I want to do and not feel guilty about my decisions. Cameron is not a destination. He's a detour." That's what she told herself, although her fierce need for him made it feel less so. "Not everyone I get involved with has to be husband material. Mother isn't always right."

"Not always, but often," Ella said in quiet resignation.

She'd married, but not someone their mother considered "suitable" for her station in life. When the marriage didn't last, Sylvie wasted no time saying *I told you so*.

Studying Ella now, Simone wondered if her sister had ever been happy in her marriage. Had she ever felt genuine love and affection for the man she pledged to love until death, or had it all been a mirage?

Why did so many relationships not last? Even when the spouses loved each other passionately, the way she thought Ella and her husband used to.

"I don't agree with what you're doing, but I haven't had sex in months." Ella smiled. "Have an extra orgasm for me while you're at it."

If Simone was lucky, she'd have enough to last for a very long time.

Chapter Thirteen

By the time Simone arrived, Cameron had been at home at least an hour. He left the club early, showered and changed into a pullover and jeans, and proceeded to anxiously await her arrival.

When she did arrive, she came in with a Gucci rolling suitcase, obviously prepared to spend the night. She wore black heels and a purple, floral, feminine dress with a full skirt that swirled around her ankles.

Having waited so long, Cameron felt at the end of his rope. Had it only been three and a half weeks since he made love to her? It felt much longer.

She barely had time to cross the threshold before he was on her. He had no remorse about his actions. She knew why she was there. He knew why she was there. They were both fully aware and conscious of what they were about to do and the reason they were together at that exact moment.

Cameron covered Simone's lips with his own, pushing both hands into her tumble of midnight curls and crushing her to him, his body aching with need—an undignified need to possess, consume, and devour her.

To his utmost satisfaction, her ardor matched his. Her fingers gripped the base of his spine, pressing into his bare skin underneath the cotton pullover. Fingernails scored his flesh. Moans of pleasure filled his ears as her tongue forged past his teeth and delved boldly into his mouth.

Cameron popped open the buttons at the front of the dress and revealed the white lace underneath. The bra cupped her supple breasts like a pair of hands and lifted them as if in an offering to his mouth.

Impatiently, he pressed his lips against the soft fabric and sucked one swollen nub until the material became dark and wet from his attention. Gasping, Simone clutched the back of his head and murmured his name, making an incoherent, raspy sound that was little more than a throaty whimper.

Sweeping her up into his arms like a prize, Cameron headed up the stairs to the bedroom. Inside, he removed her clothes, almost tearing the fine garment made of chiffon from her curvaceous body.

He discarded the dress in a heap to one side and then laid claim to her mouth again.

"Did you fuck him?" he asked against her mouth, hands on her waist, jealous anger building inside him. He wanted to know and didn't want to know at the same time.

Wide eyes stared back at him. "No."

The weight of worry lifted from his shoulders.

"And you…did you…with her?" She seemed to have difficulty asking the question, her breathing sounding labored and pained, shoulders tightening as she braced for the answer.

"No." Cameron reached around and unhooked the bra. "Apparently, lipstick stained my collar and my mouth. This color right here." His thumb swiped her bottom lip.

Satisfaction lit her pupils and, keeping eye contact, Simone sucked his finger between her ruby-tinted lips, swirling her tongue around the tip in a tantalizing tease that sent a pang of hunger through his loins.

Stepping back, she let the bra fall to her wrists, tossed it into a corner, and stood before him, a goddess enveloped in beautiful brown skin, wearing nothing but a pair of white lace panties and heels.

He stripped off the shirt, and she touched him, raking her nails over his firm skin and letting her fingertips glide through the soft hairs that arrowed down to the waistband of his trousers.

"I want to taste every inch of you, Cam," Simone whispered, releasing the button on his jeans.

The sound of the zipper lowering mingled with the sounds of their uneven breathing. Then Simone sank to her knees on the plush rug before him and dragged the jeans past his lean hips, past his muscular thighs, all the way to his ankles. She kissed his hips, the heat of his boner pressing like a hot brand into her cheek.

Licking the inside of his thighs, she heard the sharp intake of breath—a sudden, involuntary sound.

Then her tongue traced from the base to the tip, dragging a hard groan from the depths of Cameron's chest. Clasping his thickness in one hand, Simone sucked the tip between her lips, and while keeping her tongue broad, slid her mouth up and down his shaft. He groaned and placed a hand on her head.

The fingers in her hair trembled slightly as they curled into the tresses. But she continued to move, using her mouth to bring him pleasure while stroking the inside of his thighs.

Swearing viciously, Cameron's short, labored pants filled the room while she worked him in her mouth. Biting his lip, he moved his hips slightly, gliding in and out of her mouth. The noises he made turned her on and filled her with satisfaction, and she grew wet with anticipation of when their bodies would be joined.

Swearing again, louder this time, Cameron thrust his hips faster. "Sweetheart…"

Simone heard the warning in his voice. She knew what it meant. But she ignored it, moving her mouth more rapidly over him. Sucking harder.

Looking up, her gaze met his. His eyes were a dark swirl of chocolate, his face contorted into a pleasure-filled grimace as he gripped the back of her neck and bit down hard on his bottom lip.

At last, his head lolled back and with a violent shudder, his mouth fell open on a throaty, guttural roar. Gasping, he unleashed into the back of her throat while his hand held her head in an almost painful grasp.

Cameron collapsed onto the bed on his back, breathing heavily. His chest heaved. His eyes remained shut as he savored the remnants of bliss.

Simone kicked off her heels, tugged the denim pants completely off his legs, and wiggled out of her panties.

"You like?" she asked, smiling to herself.

Cameron pulled her on top of him. "You couldn't tell?"

Her soft feminine form glided over his body, her hands wreaking havoc as they ran over his pecs and down to his abs. Heat washed over his skin. Every single inch of him was aware and alive and attuned to her touch.

When her hand reached between his legs, his shaft immediately began to harden, growing longer and harder as she massaged it back to life.

He sucked air between his teeth. "Goddamn, woman."

He spread his fingers wide and ran them down her spine all the way to her bottom and squeezed. He kissed her throat and then rolled her onto her back so he could take the tip of one breast into his mouth. Her breasts were amazing. Full and soft. The dark tips seemed to fit perfectly to his mouth, and her moans of pleasure only served to urge him on. He went from one to the other, gorging to his fill, refusing to stop even when she squirmed and begged for a break.

Finally, sheathed in a condom, Cameron lay poised above her on his elbows. One thigh scissored between her smooth legs and he thrust his hips downward. She lifted toward him—ready, eager.

"Cam…"

He could never get enough of her saying his name like that.

"I got you," he whispered.

He kissed her throat again. Her lips. Her eyes. Her brows.

He moved. Long, deep strokes.

She clung to him. Meeting each thrust.

Cameron lifted one of her legs and angled his hips. Goddamn, she felt so good. Too good. It took great effort to hold back and not explode the way he ached to.

But he held on. Working his hips. Sliding through the slick heat until she cried out and convulsed around him. Even then he continued to hold on—pushing his body to the limits of restraint until she stiffened into a tight arch beneath him as another orgasm ripped through her frame.

Watching her lose control—head tossed back, eyes closed—finally made him yield to the pressure and come undone. The climax sliced up his spine, his ass contracting as he plunged one more time into the ecstasy between her legs.

Cameron collapsed on the middle of the bed and pulled Simone with him. He wrapped his arms around her and held her tight. He didn't want to move. He didn't want to let her go.

Simone murmured something unintelligible and settled half on top of him. Tucked under his chin, one arm thrown across his chest, her even breaths fanned his skin in a slow, constant rhythm.

Cameron's lids grew heavy in the dark. The restless energy that had plagued him for weeks was now long gone. Kissing Simone's damp forehead, he ran a hand over her back and side and hips. He never wanted to move from this position. He could stay like this indefinitely, their brown limbs intertwined, and their bodies seared together as if they were still one.

Chapter Fourteen

The sharp cry of the ringing telephone pierced the veil of sleep, and Simone stretched and mumbled her displeasure at the interruption. She eased away from Cameron's warm body as he stretched across the big bed and answered the phone.

"Hello?"

Simone watched his profile in the dark room. He listened for a moment and then cursed.

"Anybody hurt?" The person on the other end answered the question. "Well, that's good. I'll be right there." He hung up and sighed heavily, running a weary hand down his face.

"What's wrong?" Simone asked.

"There's been an incident at the club. A guy named Reeve pulled a knife on our bartender, Josh, when he went on break."

Simone gasped and raised onto an elbow. "Oh no. Is everybody okay?"

"Josh is fine, but the perpetrator got injured in the scuffle. Police and medics are on their way."

"How did he get a knife into the club?"

Cameron shook his head. "Believe me, where there's a will, there's a way. Every time we employ a new security measure, some asshole tries to find a way to circumvent it. It's a constant battle to stay one step ahead. This Reeve guy apparently had a problem with Josh because he feels he stole his girl. He's been hanging around the club, just watching, night after night. Fortunately, our security had been keeping an eye on him, so when he made his move, they were right there."

He got out of the bed and flicked on the light in the walk-in closet. Simone heard him moving around and wasn't sure what to do. Should she stay here, or leave with him?

The answer to that question was resolved when Cameron came out of the closet, tucking a dress shirt into his pants. "Hopefully, this won't take too long to resolve. Mason's not much of a talker, and I personally prefer to talk to the police. I should be back in a couple of hours."

Cameron ducked back into the closet and flicked out the light. He stuck his arms in the sleeves of a black jacket and leaned across the bed. He brought his face so close to hers she could see his eyes in the dark.

"Make sure you're here when I get back," he said in a low voice, his gaze steady.

"I'm not going anywhere," Simone promised.

He dropped a kiss to her lips and left, quietly sliding the door into place.

Alone, Simone smiled in the darkness and tugged the sheet up around her shoulders, burrowing into the warmth Cameron left behind on the linens and pillows.

At some point she must have fallen asleep again, because the next thing she knew, she felt movement on the bed when Cameron returned.

She groaned grumpily.

"Sorry I woke you." He pulled her close from behind and nuzzled her neck, pushing one hair-sprinkled thigh between her legs.

Simone yawned and stretched, sleepily reaching back for him in the dark. Her hand landed on his firm, naked butt.

"Did you get everything resolved?" she asked.

"Yeah. We had to file a report. The usual stuff when there's an incident like that."

"Any problems with the police?"

"No, but I wasn't too worried. I have a good relationship with the chief, and we give officers special treatment when they come through."

"You have them wrapped around your finger?" she teased, though she wouldn't be surprised. Look at how easily he'd managed to get her at his beck and call. She hadn't thought twice about coming over when he asked. She'd only hesitated because she didn't want to seem too eager.

Cameron chuckled, and his warm breath brushed the back of her neck. "Nothing like that. It's just that in this business, you have to have a good rapport with the police. Especially when incidents like this occur. They wield a lot of power, but because they know us and we have a good relationship with them, they allowed us to keep the club open the rest of the night and minimized the disturbance by taking Reeve out the back instead of the front." He yawned.

"I'm glad," Simone said. "You sound tired."

"I am."

She twisted around to face him and flung one leg over his hip and an arm around his neck. She planted a gentle kiss on his forehead near the edge of his hairline. "Get some sleep." She massaged his neck with her fingertips and the heel of her hand.

Cameron groaned. "That feels good."

"It would feel much better if I could stand behind you and do it right, but this will have to do. It's a trick my masseur uses to help me relax." She continued the movements for a few minutes longer until the tension left his muscles. Then she smoothed a hand over his back.

Cameron nestled his face into her neck. "You have anywhere to be in the morning?"

"No."

"Good."

She didn't think it was possible, but he somehow he managed to pull her closer.

A few minutes later, Cameron placed a kiss to her collarbone. "I could get used to this," he said quietly.

"Get used to what?" Simone said groggily. She was slipping fast into sleep again.

"Coming home at night to you in my bed."

Simone's eyes popped open, and she stared into the darkness, her heart beating a little faster. She understood the way he felt. Lying in his bed, waiting for him, had felt like the most natural thing in the world—as if she'd been doing it for years. And now, with his pelvis pressed solidly between her legs, they were as close as two people could be without being joined physically.

With her heart feeling as if it was about to explode, she closed her eyes and whispered, "I could get used to it, too."

Chapter Fifteen

Simone woke to the scent of coffee and sausage. For the third Sunday in a month—having missed one because of travel—she awoke to the smell of one of Cameron's breakfasts.

Smiling, she inhaled deeply and stretched before hopping out of bed, but instead of getting the clothes she'd brought, went to his dresser. Rummaging through the drawers, she found a gray V-neck T-shirt, perfect for lounging around the loft on a lazy Sunday morning, and a pair of burgundy drawstring running shorts she'd seen him wear on a jog around the neighborhood.

Simone slipped the soft T-shirt over her head, dragged on a thong, and slipped on his pants. The clothes swallowed her, but she always preferred to wear his than the ones she brought. After brushing her teeth and washing up, she pulled her thick mane into a loose ponytail with a rhinestone ponytail holder and then padded down the stairs in search of Cameron.

She found him reading the paper in the middle of the sofa, sipping coffee with his feet propped on the low table in front of him. Hair dusted his cheeks and jaw because he hadn't shaved yet, and he wore a pair of black sweats and his reading glasses, his bare chest exposed to her appreciative eyes.

When he heard her, he looked up and scanned her attire. A small smile, one of approval, tugged at the corners of his lips before he dived back into the article. "Why don't you ever wear the clothes you bring?"

"I'd rather wear yours." Simone headed into the kitchen and the scent of pork and eggs greeted her. "Smells good in here."

"Figured you'd be hungry when you woke up after I put it down last night. Again."

Simone giggled, shaking her head. "I am." She poured herself a cup of coffee and went into the living room with a plate of eggs, sausage, and strawberries.

She settled down beside him and ate quietly while he read. Everything was delicious, of course. The eggs were scrambled soft with cheese, the way she liked, and the coffee flavorful and strong. "Ethiopian blend?" she asked, holding up the cup.

"Yep," Cameron answered.

She finished her meal and set aside the plate and coffee cup. She peered at the article, a story about the changing business landscape in Atlanta and the opportunities for entrepreneurs. "No one gets the paper anymore."

"I do."

"Did you know you could get newspapers and magazines electronically now? They're called digital subscriptions." Once again, she thought about how old-fashioned he was, an old soul in a young body.

He looked at her. "Are you being smart?"

"Me?" she said with false innocence.

He smiled at her. "Gimme a kiss."

She gladly obliged, leaning into his warm skin and giving him a sweet, prolonged morning kiss.

"You taste like coffee, scrambled eggs, and sausage," he murmured.

"And strawberries," she added.

"That, too."

Simone giggled and flicked her tongue against his mouth. She couldn't help but laugh when she was with Cameron. Simply being in his presence made her happy. She kissed his neck and then his hair-roughened cheek, unable to resist being affectionate with him. He grumbled, but she knew he liked it.

In retrospect, she'd never truly experienced these tender, intimate gestures of affection with the men she dated. They always behaved more like acquaintances—there to fill the time and the needs of her body. But Cameron filled her heart and relaxed her spirit.

She didn't want to complain because she knew she lived a life of untold wealth, privilege, and opportunities not afforded to the less fortunate. Nonetheless, she appreciated this simpler life where she didn't have to worry about being Simone Brooks. Always on, performing for prying eyes, unable to make the smallest misstep without being castigated in the press or by "well-meaning" family members.

With Cameron, she was free. Not restricted or stifled because of her position and family legacy. Free to wear drawstring shorts and comfy T-shirts, and she didn't have to be perfect, dress perfectly, wear makeup all the time, none of that. Cameron accepted her in her many forms. And while the sex was great, being here with him, and allowed to loosen up and be silly, were equally important.

"What are we doing today?" she asked, resting her chin on his shoulder.

"I need to go to the supermarket. And…we could check out some furniture."

Her head popped up. "Furniture? For what?"

"This place." He tossed aside the newspaper and flung an arm over the back of the sofa. "I saw a set I'd like to buy, and I want to get your opinion."

Simone settled closer to his side and glanced around the room. "Hmm…good idea."

He cleared his throat loudly.

"I just mean that you could use an update," she said quickly.

He chuckled. "Yeah, I know. When I lived with a roommate, all the furniture belonged to him, and my parents gave me all this when they downsized so I'd have something to sit on when I moved in. It's time to finally get new pieces, and since you're here…"

"You figured you could use my expertise."

"Expertise? Ha."

Cameron rose from the seat, taking the comfortable heat of his body with him.

"Don't be difficult, Cam. You know you need my expertise. My mother designs furniture, after all. Her eye for design and layout rubbed off on me."

"I guess we'll see, won't we?"

Simone was excited that he actually wanted to get her opinion on the furniture he was going to decorate his house with and would not let his smart aleck comments quell her excitement. "When are we leaving?" she asked.

"In thirty minutes." Cameron picked up the empty mugs and her plate and went into the kitchen.

"Thirty minutes! You know I need thirty minutes to take a shower."

"You're going to have to cut that short today, sweetheart."

"I have to get clean, Cam." She followed and stood at the window of the kitchen, watching him put the dishes in the dishwasher.

"Do you have more dirt on your body than everybody else? Ten minutes, max, is all you need."

"You're insane."

"If you take longer than ten minutes, I'm leaving you."

"You can't. You said you need my help."

"Watch me."

"You're awful." Simone crossed her arms over her chest.

Cameron sauntered out of the kitchen and came to stand in front of her. "Look at you pouting. You act that way because you've gotten your way your whole life." His gaze lowered to her breasts, where the nipples protruded at the front of his shirt. "If you want more time, you're going to have to pay for it."

Her ears perked up. "Oh, really?" Simone stuck out her breasts even more.

"Mmm-hmm." He lifted the tail of the shirt and palmed her waist, pulling her close enough to encounter the semi-erect bulge at the front of his pants.

"So how do you expect me to pay for those extra twenty minutes?" Simone whispered, her loins tingling in response to the close contact.

"You'll have to pay for them on your back," he replied with a wolfish grin.

"Cam!"

"Cam!" he mocked. He kissed her neck and sucked gently on the skin. "It's your fault for looking so sexy in my clothes. How am I supposed to be good with you walking around like this, hmm? No bra. Skin so soft. Smelling good."

Simone rested her forehead against his chest and inhaled the manly scent of his skin. He paid her compliments all the time. Spontaneous and unprovoked words of affection, even when she didn't feel she looked her best, like today, with her hair uncombed, no makeup, and not a designer label in sight. She would have to think of a way to make him feel good, too. To demonstrate how deeply she cared for and appreciated him.

He plucked an earlobe into her mouth.

"Cam," Simone moaned, arching her throat and lifting her arms around his neck.

He drew a sharp breath. "I love the way you say my name." He ran his hands slowly down her back and grabbed her ass.

Her heart soared as he lifted her from the floor, and her legs quickly and automatically wrapped around his waist.

An energetic kiss ensued when she closed her mouth over his—a kiss that had Simone grinding against him and left them both groaning and breathless.

Cameron looked at her with slits for eyes. "Sex first, then furniture, then groceries. Sound like a plan?"

"Best plan I've ever heard."

Letting out a deep, throaty laugh, he proceeded to climb the stairs with her still wrapped around him.

Chapter Sixteen

With her hand tucked securely in Cameron's, Simone strolled through the ginormous furniture outlet. In the month since they'd been seeing each other regularly, they'd fallen into a routine that fit their opposing schedules. When they could, they spent mornings and weekdays together. Simone scheduled her appointments as late in the day as she could, so she could leave his loft as late as possible before starting the day.

Some nights they ate dinner together before he went to work, and she stayed behind to catch up on foundation business—sending emails, setting appointments, and reviewing financials. By the time he got off in the wee hours of the morning, she was asleep, but when he climbed into the bed, the movement always woke her up. She would pout and complain because she hated her sleep being disturbed. Then he'd brush the hair from the back of her neck and shush her with delicate kisses until she snuggled into his warm embrace and fell back asleep.

Shopping was another one of the routine tasks they did together. He was very particular about the ingredients he used in the meals he prepared, and she'd seen him argue quite passionately about produce at the farmer's market. It turned her on that a man so rugged and outdoorsy had such a caring side, where he insisted on feeding the people he cared about only the best available.

They'd even developed a comfortable rhythm in the kitchen, where they took turns being executive chef and sous chef, exploring new dishes and experimenting with textures and flavors. He showed her proper knife technique and offered tips and shortcuts on processes in the kitchen. His constant encouragement and patience gave her the confidence to try new recipes and branch out from the basics.

"You're back." A salesman wearing a gray suit approached with a big smile and his hand extended.

Cameron shook his hand. "I brought my lady with me this time to get her opinion."

My lady. That was the first time he'd used that term to describe her, and Simone blushed with pleasure.

"Hello, I'm Brent." The man's voice blasted across the short distance and with an engaging smile attached.

"Simone." She smiled back.

"Come on, let's go check out your furniture," Brent said, jerking his head toward the back of the store.

The showroom contained contemporary and traditional pieces bearing huge signs with the regular prices slashed through, and the low prices big, bright, and bold. Simone had come to learn that Cameron was very conservative when it came to spending money. He'd lived with a roommate for years to save for the ideal home in a hot and trendy part of town. Now that he was ready to get furniture, it made sense that he was taking his time, trying to find the perfect collection for the place he called home.

"How's your daughter doing?" Cameron asked Brent, as they followed.

Simone eyed the different furniture groupings, making mental notes as they walked along.

"We have a few more surgeries before the doctors think she'll completely recover, but you know how it is. Everything costs so damn much." He glanced at Simone over his shoulder. "Pardon my language."

"It's okay. If you don't mind my asking, what's wrong with your daughter?"

"A few years ago, she was burned pretty badly in a fire in a newly built home my wife and I bought. The investigators said it was faulty wiring, and we've been fighting with the builder for the past couple of years to get them to pay. They refuse to admit any wrongdoing. Our insurance covers most of the medical bills, but not all, and my daughter's being treated by a specialist in Texas. The flights back and forth, the hotel stays, everything—it's adding up." He swallowed and let out a puff of air. "All I care about is making sure my kid feels better, you know?"

Simone nodded her understanding. "I work for a foundation that may be able to help. Do you have a card?" she asked.

Brent stopped walking and glanced between her and Cameron. "Really? I sure do." He pulled a card from inside his jacket and handed it to her.

"I can't promise anything. You'd have to fit within program guidelines, but I can certainly look into it and have someone get back to you."

His face lit up with hope. "Thank you, I appreciate that so much. You have no idea."

"I'm not promising you anything," Simone said cautiously.

"I understand, I understand. I appreciate you even trying." Brent grinned. "All right, you came here to talk furniture. Let's do that." He pointed at a set. "This is the one you were interested in, right?" he asked Cameron.

"This is it," Cameron confirmed.

Simone pursed her lips at the collection of heavy chairs in dark leather and tables in mahogany wood. "It's nice…"

"But?" Both men said.

"You have a lot of space to fill," she said to Cameron. "And…I think your place could use a little warmth and light. How about…" She turned in a semicircle, scanning the open space. Pointing, she said, "Those pillows. You can take the two leather sofas, but soften them with that purple chaise lounge over there. After all, purple is your favorite color. Then…" She tapped her lips and turned again, her gaze flicking over various pieces. "When we came in, I saw a tan loveseat that would look nice with that chocolate chair and a few pillows. Add another table and some furnishings, and you have two sitting areas. One near the window and near your office alcove in front of the fireplace." She placed both hands on her hips and waited for feedback.

"Actually, she makes a good point." Brent looked back and forth at the various options Simone pointed out.

"Would it be a problem for me to mix and match like that?" Cameron asked.

"Not at all. We can make it work."

"And it creates a more eclectic look, which is perfect for the loft," Simone added.

Cameron nodded slowly. "I think you're right." A broad grin spread across his face.

Simone eased over and slipped an arm around his waist. "Lucky you, I was available to lend my expertise."

"Yes, lucky me." He dropped a kiss to her mouth. "All right, Brent. Thanks a lot."

"Are we getting the furniture today?" Brent asked hopefully.

"I need to pick out a few more things, find some accent pieces. And I need to get rid of the furniture I have now. I'll sell it or give it away or something. So…I'll give you a call in a few weeks?"

"Sounds good. I'll make a note of everything you liked here."

Hand in hand, Cameron and Simone scoured the showroom. They didn't find other pieces he could use, so they took a trip to two more stores, choosing light fixtures and accent tables.

By the time they finished, Simone was exhausted but oddly exhilarated. Normally, she would have had a designer or her assistant handle shopping details, but spending the day with Cameron made her feel like she was part of a couple.

Every time he used the word "we" in reference to the choices for his loft, her insides did a happy dance. And even though she was doing things she wouldn't normally, with a man she never thought she'd be so content with, for the first time in a long time she felt she might be on the right track.

Chapter Seventeen

Cameron took a good look at his reflection in the full-length mirror in his bedroom. The tuxedo fit perfectly. But of course it did. It was Italian and custom made for him, all of which had been paid for by Simone. The tailor she chose sent over the tux, along with a pair of black Italian-made shoes.

This wasn't the first time Simone had plunked down a heap of money for a gift, but it was certainly the most money she'd spent so far. The gold money clip and high-end wireless headphones were nothing compared to this entire ensemble.

He rolled his neck, trying to release the tension and unease he felt about the fact that his woman had paid for his clothes. Thousands of dollars, no less.

"Shake it off, Cam."

Money was no object to Simone, and while he certainly wasn't poor, he still had to get used to the idea of spending the kind of cash she did. His sister, Harper, tended to spend quite a bit of money, too, but her spending habits were nothing compared to Simone's, a woman who rode around the city with a driver, employed a personal assistant, and spent an exorbitant amount on everything from clothes to cosmetics. Meanwhile, he had put off buying furniture for a whole year because he didn't want to go into debt, and then the furniture he intended to buy, while high end, was marked down at an outlet store. He couldn't imagine Simone ever walking into an outlet store and buying anything.

His most extravagant expenditures were his house, which he managed to get at a good price because it was a foreclosure, and his Lexus SUV, his dream car and a gift to himself for accomplishing his goal with his siblings of making Club Masquerade such a success.

Tonight he and Simone were on their way to the Fox Theatre where her mother was screening a documentary and having a fundraiser. The documentary provided an uncensored report about the outdated practice of child brides still prevalent in some parts of the world. Tonight's fundraiser would bring attention to the devastating effects of this practice, and fund economic and education initiatives that would benefit the young girls. Simone wanted to go not only to support her mother, but because it was one of the projects she worked on at the Johnson Foundation.

The phone beside the bed rang. When he answered, Simone said, "I'm downstairs."

"I'll be down in a few."

Cameron shook off the hesitation, left the loft, and met her downstairs. A limo idled in front of the building with Simone's driver standing beside it. When Cameron appeared, the man opened the door and he climbed in. Within seconds, they were on their way.

Simone looked amazing in a shimmery gold one-shoulder dress that clasped her hourglass figure, and diamond earrings so long they touched her shoulders. He'd lost track of all the jewelry she owned. She seemed to own a piece to match every article of clothing in her closet.

She chose a simple hairstyle tonight, parted on one side and pulled back into a neat bun. She often complained about her hair— its thickness and the long hours her personal stylist spent washing and drying it. But he loved her hair. Especially when the raven strands spread out across his pillows in moments of unguarded laughter, or unbridled passion as his body plunged into hers, each thrust fighting to quench the unchecked desire she evoked every time she came near.

"Why are you looking at me like that?" she asked.

"Thinking about how beautiful you are and how lucky I am," Cameron answered.

She smiled at the compliment, all dimples and pearly white teeth. "You deserve a kiss for that," she said, and placed a gentle one on his mouth as a reward.

"Mmm. Thank you." Cameron tugged the lapel of the tuxedo. "What do you think?"

"You look perfect, but there's one thing missing." She opened her hand and displayed two russet-brown cufflinks resting in her palm. "You can thank Adele for finding these. They're Tateossian cufflinks. Eighteen karat gold and finished with dinosaur bone."

Surely he didn't hear her correctly. "Did you say dinosaur bone? You're kidding, right?"

"No, it's real dinosaur bone."

Apparently, wearing the bones of a prehistoric animal was no big deal to her. Meanwhile, he was speechless.

Her cell phone rang and he stared at the cufflinks in his hand. How much did these things cost? Four hundred dollars? Five? He didn't even want to know.

He removed the ones he wore and slipped the new cufflinks into the holes at his wrists. Simone spent the rest of the ride on the phone, talking to her mother about the list of guests, all of whom sounded very important.

At one point, she sent him an apologetic grimace and he smiled reassuringly, wordlessly letting her know he understood. Even though Simone was there to support her mother, she planned to make full use of her time by networking with the donors on hand.

Fundraising was work. Work she enjoyed, but work nonetheless. Tonight he'd have a chance to see her in her element, and meet her mother and siblings.

Simone had warned him about the spectacle he could expect, but he was still ill-prepared for the flash of cameras and the people who constantly approached in an effort to get her attention. Cameron held back and let her work, blinded by the sea of jewelry, designer gowns, and tuxedos, and quietly grateful she had purchased the clothes for him, even if it did make him a little uncomfortable.

Eventually they made their way to the table where her sister Ella and brothers Reese and Stephan sat.

"Nice to meet you," he said, greeting each of them with a shake of the hand.

They were all three friendly but cautious—quietly observing after each introduction.

Her mother sat at the head table with the filmmakers. Eventually, the director and producer spoke to the audience about their project, giving an explanation of why they chose this subject matter, the process, and obstacles they faced while filming. At the very end they introduced their benefactor—Sylvie Johnson—and thanked her for believing in the project.

With a glowing introduction, Sylvie took the stage to a round of applause. She was the epitome of style and elegance in a floor length, sleeveless gown littered with jewels, and even more in her ears, on her wrists, and around her neck. She only spoke for a few minutes about her work and support of projects other investors considered unmarketable, but when she finished, she received a standing ovation.

The meal of prime rib and truffled potatoes smelled and tasted delicious. But halfway through dinner, Cameron lost his appetite listening to the somber-faced girls discuss their plight on film. Not even the narrator's explanation that these practices are often initiated as a form of protection or to ensure the girls' economic security could get him to eat another bite.

At the end of the evening, the lights went up, and that's when he finally met Simone's people. The rich and very rich.

The night would have gone better if everyone didn't seem so concerned about what he did for a living. The questions started right away.

"Bennett…" an older woman said in a nasal voice. "Are you one of the Bennetts from California, who own the vineyards?"

"No. I'm a Georgia Bennett."

Simone placed a hand on his biceps. "He owns Club Masquerade. It's the hottest nightclub in Atlanta."

From then on, every time Simone introduced him and spoke about his work, she said exactly the same thing.

He owns Club Masquerade. It's the hottest nightclub in Atlanta.

As if the qualifying sentence was a necessity. His gaze settled on her animated face as she chatted with an older man with a walrus beard.

Was it a necessity for her? After all, everyone he met either owned businesses that brought in hundreds of millions of dollars, or had inherited their wealth. His financial status was nowhere near the level of these people.

"So this is Cameron Bennett. Finally, we meet. I'm Simone's mother." Sylvie smiled up at him, but her eyes were rather assessing. Scoping out his clothes and apparently finding them satisfactory, her smile broadened. "It's a pleasure to finally meet you."

"I feel the same. Now I see where Simone gets her beauty from. It's in the genes."

The few times he'd used that line in the past, women blushed and giggled. Not Sylvie. She simply kept the same smile on her face, as if he hadn't said a word that warranted a reaction. Which further reinforced the perception that he was being assessed.

"What did you think of the documentary?"

It was hard to relax when he felt as if every word was being picked apart.

"I thought it was excellent. Thought-provoking. Made me wish I could do more."

"Well, you can. This is a fundraiser after all, and all donations are welcome. None are too small."

Not once did the pleasant smile on her face shift, but Cameron recognized a veiled barb when he heard one.

"I'll be sure to make one before I leave."

"Wonderful. We can never do too much to help the less fortunate. If you'll excuse me I should continue to mingle. We must do lunch one day, you and I." She pressed her cheek to Simone's. "Bye-bye, my darling. Thank you so much for coming."

"Of course, Mother."

Simone and Cameron stayed a little longer and then went back to his place.

****

Simone braced one hand on the dining table and removed her shoes one by one. She moaned softly. Normally Cameron would offer to rub her feet but he wasn't in the mood tonight.

"Did you enjoy yourself?" she asked, looking hopeful.

"It was okay." He still wasn't sure how he felt.

The fundraiser was the first formal event they'd attended together. Usually they hung out at the loft or did some mundane task like go to the supermarket together. He took more nights off at the club so he could take her out, but their date nights tended to be simple events with significantly less pomp and circumstance. One evening, for instance, they attended an outdoor movie at the park with a picnic basket replete with wine, cold cuts, and other easy-to-manage snacks. Another time they went to a blues concert, and still another, they went to a comedy club and spent the entire night laughing at the antics of a local comedian.

"It takes some getting used to, but this is what I do all the time."

Cameron removed the tux jacket and tossed it on a chair. "Why do you feel the need to tell everyone I run the hottest club in Atlanta?"

A small frown whisked across Simone's forehead for a second before disappearing. "Because you do."

"Is that the only reason?"

"What do you mean?"

"You know, people there own vineyards. Your mother owns several successful businesses. I just get the feeling that you needed to brag about something."

"I wanted to brag about you. Would you prefer that I not tell people you run a club?" She seemed genuinely perplexed, and he wondered if he was overreacting. But he pressed on.

"Would you prefer not to have to tell them?"

Simone threaded her fingers together and watched him in silence for a moment. "If you're picking a fight with me, I'd like to know why."

So would he.

"You obviously did not have a good time," Simone said.

"I did."

"No, you didn't. If you're not comfortable attending these events, it's fine. Instead of taking you as an escort, I'll go alone."

"I didn't say you should do that."

"Well, what do you want, Cam? I can't change who I am or who my family is or who the people are that I spend time with." Her eyes flashed angrily at him.

"There's no need to blow up."

"I'm a little irritated because I did my best to make this easy for you."

He took two steps toward her. "Easy for me?" The way she said that rubbed him the wrong way.

"Yes. I mean, you wanted to *rent* a tux."

He laughed. "So...I would have embarrassed you if I walked up in there in a rented tux, is that right?"

She folded her hands together in a prayer-like position. "What I mean is—"

"Please, tell me what you mean."

"We have a certain…lifestyle…a certain…image to maintain." She seemed to choose her words carefully. "You could be a part of that."

"Oh, so I should be grateful? Is that what you're saying? You're doing me a favor by—what? Upgrading me?"

"You're twisting my words."

"I'm not twisting shit. You bought my clothes—and *dinosaur* cufflinks, like I'm a kept man. I'm my own man."

He stalked into the kitchen and grabbed a beer from the fridge, laughing to himself when he saw the Full Moon label. The beer her family made. Perfect. He slammed the bottle on the counter without taking a drink.

Behind him, Simone spoke through the pass-through. "I can see you're not in the mood for company tonight, so I'll call my driver and leave."

Call my driver.

Even those words, ones she'd said many times before, irritated him.

Cameron swung around and Simone was already on the way to the door. She had put her shoes back on because he heard the heels land hard on the floor as she walked.

"Simone!"

He remained in the kitchen for two seconds longer before he rushed after her. She was almost to the elevator when he caught up and caged her against the wall with hands on either side of her shoulders. She wouldn't look at him, staring down the hall with her lips pressed together in a taut line, as if fighting the urge to cry.

"Don't leave. Don't call your driver." He spoke quietly. "I'm not used to this. This life you live is…" A sigh. "I'm a simple man. I like simple things. Vinyl records. Old furniture. Rented tuxes." He sighed again and using a finger, twisted her face around to his. He looked into her watery brown eyes, and his abs contracted at the hurt he saw reflected there. He rested his forehead against hers. "I'm falling in love with you."

That was only part of the problem. He was not only falling in love, he was falling in love with a woman clearly out of his league.

Simone inhaled sharply.

"This wasn't supposed to happen," Cameron said.

Swallowing, she splayed her fingers over his chest. "From the minute I saw you, you caught my attention." She bit her lip. "When

I left your loft after that first night, I felt…incomplete. Like I was leaving a part of myself behind. When I'm not with you, when I can't see you, I feel so empty. I just…*ache*."

He felt the same way—unsettled and hollow without her.

"I want this to work," she said.

"It will."

She stared down at the floor. "I don't know. The women in my family don't have much luck with men."

"Then you'll be the first to change that."

Her gaze met his again, and in her eyes, he saw confusion at the enormity of their feelings, and a burgeoning love that excited but terrified with its swiftness and intensity.

"Your world is different from mine," Cameron said. "But I want to fit in. Forgive me?"

She touched his jaw with gentle fingers. "Yes," she whispered.

He kissed her forehead, took her by the hand, and led her back into the loft.

Chapter Eighteen

When the doorbell rang, Cameron looked up from his desk. He wasn't expecting any company, and Simone was in New York for the next couple of days.

"Just a minute," he called.

It was a little after noon, and he'd been working from home most of the day, catching up on month-end financials. Revenue at the club ticked up a little last month, thanks in part to an internationally known guest deejay one Thursday night, and the album release party for a popular rap group. All of which meant they could afford to funnel more cash into advertising and publicity this month.

He tugged on the gray shirt hanging over the back of his desk chair and went to the door. The last person he expected to see stood on the other side.

He opened the door to Sylvie Johnson. He hadn't been lying when he pointed out that he saw where Simone got her great genes from. Her mother's brown face was perfectly made up, but it was obvious she was naturally pretty, with her shiny black hair pulled back into a thick bundle at her nape.

"Hello, Cameron, do you mind if I come in?" She spoke in a pleasant voice and rested a hand on her chest, two of her fingers decorated with diamond-studded rings.

"Simone isn't here," Cameron said, although he doubted that's why Sylvie stood outside his door.

"I know Simone is not here. I came to speak to you. Do you have a few minutes to spare? I promise I won't keep you long."

Against his better judgment, Cameron allowed her into his home.

Her red-bottomed shoes clicked on the hardwood floors as she walked slowly into the expansive space, and Cameron saw where Simone got her hip-swinging walk, as well.

His shoulders tightened in apprehension, and he wished he'd already replaced the old furniture.

She stood in the middle of the floor and did a three-sixty turn, ending up facing him again.

"Have you been here long?" she asked.

"Little over a year," he answered.

"Simone told me you're getting new furniture soon. Is that correct?"

"Yes, it is."

"It will really spruce the place up."

He didn't even know how to respond to that.

"May I sit down?" Sylvie asked.

Without waiting for a response, she walked over to the area nearest the window and sat on a sofa. She gestured to the armchair across from her. "Please, sit down. I'm not here as an enemy. I'm here as a friend."

Somehow he doubted that.

Cameron sat in the chair but his body remained tense and alert for what was to come next.

"How are you?" she asked.

"With all due respect, Mrs. Brooks—"

"Miss Johnson. That's my family's name. I dropped my ex-husband's name after we divorced years ago."

"With all due respect, Miss Johnson, I was in the middle of working, so I would appreciate if you'd let me know what this is about."

"I like that. A man who gets straight to the point. Very well." She crossed one leg over the other. "My number one priority is to always protect my children. When you have children of your own, you'll understand. I worry about them every day." The smile on her face tightened a fraction. "I came by to talk to you about your relationship with my daughter. Simone is an adult, and she can see whomever she pleases. She can make her own decisions and does not need her mother's permission to date who she wants." She leaned forward. "She told me that you said you're falling in love with her."

Cameron froze on the edge of the seat.

"Don't be surprised. Simone and I talk almost every day. We're very close." She sat back, pushing her lips into a perfect little moue of deep thought. "Before I met you, she told me all about your wonderful qualities. The way you rub her feet. How you make sure to have plenty of bananas at your home because it's her favorite fruit to snack on. It's all very sweet. I appreciate it so much, because you see, I know how special my daughter is." She interlaced her fingers atop her knees. "She would make some lucky man the perfect wife. Simone is beautiful. Intelligent. And very caring. To a fault, really." She laughed throatily. "When she was ten, she came to me and her father with all her birthday money and presents and had us donate them to a children's home. That same year, she forged a check with my signature and sent thousands of dollars to a family in need that she'd seen on the news. The bank notified me of the forgery, and I ended up honoring the check, but as you can imagine, I realized I had to rein in her benevolence and give her proper direction. So from a very young age, she started volunteering her time with programs the family foundation sponsors, and now that's what she does all day—making sure the less fortunate receive the financial help they need to survive or get the necessities of life." She paused. "But sadly, I feel that her generous nature can also be a flaw."

"No one can be too generous," Cameron said, wondering where the conversation was going.

"That's not true," Sylvie said in a singsong voice, wagging her finger. "One must be prudent in one's generosity. Simone would give a stranger the clothes off her back, if she could. And that's dangerous. People like her, if they're not careful, can easily be taken advantage of. Do you understand what I'm saying?"

"Are you accusing me of using your daughter?"

"Does it sound like I am?"

"Miss Johnson—"

"Cameron. My daughter is always looking for a cause." She looked around the room, and even though her expression didn't change, he sensed the disapproval. Her hand glided over the worn fabric of the sofa. "Simone cares deeply for you. So much so, I worry that she would neglect her own needs to please you."

"I would never ask Simone to neglect her own needs, wants, desires, or anything else that makes her happy, for me."

"Of course you wouldn't. You're not that type of person. You're a man of character."

Every compliment she paid him sounded sarcastic.

Cameron laughed softly. "Really? Because I'm getting the distinct impression that you not only think Simone sees me as a charity case, you think I'm taking advantage of her."

"I never said you're taking advantage of her," she pointed out.

"Good, because I'm not. I love her."

"Do you?"

"Yes. I'm not interested in Simone's money," Cameron said through his teeth. "I don't want anything but the best for her."

Sylvie fell silent. He wished he could read her, but the woman was a master at keeping her emotions hidden.

"And that's my dilemma." She sounded distraught, her voice strained as if she carried the weight of the world on her shoulders. "You see, as I mentioned to you before, Simone has a generous heart. If you want the best for her, then I'm sure you wouldn't want her to give up the life she's accustomed to, for you. But if you only care about the money..." She let the words trail off.

Cameron frowned. "What are you talking about?"

"My daughter and I had a very interesting conversation. She seems to think that for this relationship to work long-term, she should give up the luxuries she enjoys." Her brow wrinkled like someone with great concern.

Cameron swallowed. A burning sensation in his gut expanded and refused to disappear as he thought about all the things Simone would have to give up to be with him.

"I'm sure you can understand my concern," she continued. "No more vacations on the Amalfi coast. Did you know she goes twice a year? No more shopping trips to Milan." She examined her fingers and played with one of her rings. "No more diamonds and jewels. No more driver." She lifted her gaze. "Of course you make a good enough living for the average woman, but Simone is above average, wouldn't you say? The type of wealth she's accustomed to, you simply cannot provide. I'm sure there is a young woman out there who would be happy to have you as a husband and for whom you can provide a lifestyle that would make her happy. But the truth is, Cameron." Her face changed, her tone becoming hard. "If Simone were to...say, marry you, your relationship would be a step down for her. And is that what you really want? Do you want to be a step down?"

Cameron shot up from the chair. "You've said enough. You should leave now."

Sylvie rose at a much slower rate. "I know this is not what you wanted to hear, but it's the truth."

"Leave." With his blood boiling, he was dangerously close to grabbing her by the neck and tossing her into the hallway.

She walked slowly toward the door without a word, the sound of her high heels clacking on the floor. "I would prefer that you keep this conversation between the two of us. My children don't like me to meddle, but I'm afraid that as a mother, I can't stop helping them when I can." She turned at the door, the pleasant mask back in place. Her expression was cool, and her eyes lacked warmth. "Think about what I said. Think about what's best for both Simone *and* you. If you really love my daughter, you'll give her up. Isn't that what love is? Sacrifice? Doing what's best for the other person? Do what's best for Simone, Cameron. If you love my daughter, that's what you'll do." She tossed another glance at the interior of the loft before she met his gaze one last time. "Have a good afternoon."

And then she was gone.

Chapter Nineteen

After checking in with the general manager and floor managers, Cameron left Club Masquerade. Simone had returned from New York yesterday and he hadn't had a chance to see her and talk to her about the conversation with her mother. He wasn't even sure how to broach the topic but knew they needed to discuss her mother's visit before they flew to Miami tomorrow. He'd have to attend two formal events as her escort for the weekend.

Tugging on his tie, Cameron trudged down the hallway to his loft with a couple of folders tucked under his arm. He might do a little work later.

He spoke to Simone before he left the club to let her know he was on his way, and the call had been interesting, to say the least. She'd sounded extremely excited, and he couldn't help but wonder what was going on.

He turned the key in the lock and entered the loft, and paused on the threshold. He noticed the difference right away. Behind him, the door snicked closed, and he walked slowly into the condo. The old furniture was gone, and the entire space had been transformed with the items he and Simone had picked out at the outlet store.

"Surprise!" Simone rushed down the staircase in skin-tight designer jeans and a fuchsia silk blouse, her grin broad and eyes bright. "You came home too early. I ordered a late dinner so it could be here waiting for you, but you beat me to it." She threw her arms wide with a flourish. "Ta-dah! What do you think?"

Cameron scanned the room, noting the leather furniture, the purple chaise, and all the other tables and chairs they'd chosen in the outlet showroom, as well as the lighting and items from the other two stores. Not only that, she'd added tasteful additions, like potted plants, knickknacks, and pictures on the walls.

"What did you do with my old stuff?" he asked.

"Adele is working on selling everything, so you'll get money for all the old pieces. But all the new items you looked at and liked are here, plus a few extras." She bounced up and down on her stilettos, mighty pleased with herself. She pressed her hands together like someone about to pray. "Notice anything missing?"

His heart stopped. "Where is my record collection?"

"Don't panic. It's right here." She walked over to a new piece of furniture that his turntable sat on top of. "It's an Atocha cabinet. Walnut finished. All the records are packed in and organized for you by genre and artist name."

Cameron rubbed his forehead. Atocha was top of the line. On the low end, a small cabinet cost anywhere from four to five thousand dollars. With all the drawers of this model, it must have cost almost twice as much.

Cameron tossed his keys and the folders in his hand onto the steel table. "What are you doing?"

Simone's smile faltered. "I don't know what you mean." She appeared genuinely confused.

"You know exactly what I mean. You spent a bunch of money I didn't ask you to spend."

Her brow wrinkled. "What's the big deal? They're gifts. I can afford it."

"And I can't?"

Her mouth fell open. "That's not what I meant."

"I can buy my own furniture, Simone."

Her shoulders straightened and she placed a hand on her hip. "So you don't want anything from me, is that it?"

"That's not the point. Buying all my furniture is too much. What were you thinking? I told you I would get it myself."

"But you hadn't, so I thought…I thought maybe…" Her voice faltered again.

"You thought I couldn't afford it," Cameron supplied, his lips drawn tight.

She swallowed. "It's just furniture."

"It's not just furniture. It's thousands of dollars that you didn't even think twice about spending because you thought I couldn't afford to buy what I needed for myself." One hand clenched into a fist.

"I can't believe you're arguing with me over a gift," Simone said.

"You're not even listening to me, are you? Because you're too busy thinking about what you have to say before I finish."

Her lips parted and her face took on the shocked appearance of someone who'd been slapped. "You don't have to act like a dick, Cam. I was trying to do something nice for you."

"No, you're treating me like one of your charity cases."

"That's not true."

"No? So replacing my old furniture with new furniture is not charity? Buying me shoes and a tuxedo, so I could look presentable at the event I escort you to, is not charity?"

"We're in a relationship, and I invited you to the fundraiser, so it made sense that I would pay for your clothes. It was a very important event. You can't go in any old tux. People would talk."

"And who could forget those cufflinks."

"Why do you hate them so much? They're perfectly good cufflinks," she said, sounding defensive.

"Why does anyone need eighteen karat gold cufflinks finished with dinosaur bone, Simone? Dinosaur bone!" When he'd researched them, he discovered they cost more than twice what he'd originally thought.

The quiet in the room dragged out between them. Neither he nor Simone spoke. Neither made a move or a sound.

Finally, Simone cleared her throat. "If it'll make you feel better, then you can pay me back for the furniture," she said quietly.

Cameron stalked over to his desk and pulled out the checkbook. He dated and signed a check and then walked over to Simone and extended it to her. "Fill in the amount."

Simone took the check, the excitement long gone from her face and replaced with uncertainty. "So that's it? I should keep my filthy money to myself?" she asked.

"There's nothing wrong with your money."

"I just can't spend it on you."

Cameron heaved out a breath. "I can afford nice things, but I can't buy the things you can."

"I never asked you to, but none of that matters because my money makes you uncomfortable."

He felt like crap. Because he was hurting her and because he felt like he could never measure up. "Simone—"

"I'll stop. I won't do it anymore," she said.

"Then you'll be changing who you are."

"So what do you want me to do? I don't have to buy these things. I don't have to have these things. I don't need them. I can still do my work without all the extras."

Like her mother had said, she was willing to give up her life of luxury. For him.

"You'd be unhappy. Can you honestly tell me you wouldn't miss your designer clothes and twice-a-year trips to the Amalfi Coast?"

She bit her lip. "I would make do."

Cameron scrubbed a hand across his forehead. "I don't want you to make do, sweetheart. I don't want you to be miserable because of me. I don't want you to settle."

"I'm not settling."

"You deserve to be—"

"Are you breaking up with me?"

Cameron paused. His body immediately rejected the thought, his gut and neck tightening to the point of discomfort. But they came from different worlds. "I think we need a break. To think."

Simone took a shocked step back and pressed a hand to her chest. "Fine," she said. "It's funny, but when I set up this surprise, I wondered if you'd have a problem with the gifts. And you did. Huh. The Brooks women curse strikes again."

"What are you talking about?"

"Don't worry. It doesn't concern you," she said bitterly. She picked up her purse from a bookcase against the brick wall. "The food will be here soon. I already paid for it, so how do you want to handle that? Do you want to give me cash, or should I just add it to the balance on the check?"

"Now you're trying to be funny."

"No, absolutely not. I don't want to insult your delicate—"

She stopped abruptly and tensed when he stepped toward her but didn't move away. She looked up at him in defiance.

"I'm not delicate," Cameron said quietly.

Simone unsnapped her purse and pulled out a few large bills. "Whenever I stayed here, I used your electricity and water." She dug into her purse again, and pulled out another handful of bills. "A few more just to be safe." She tossed hundreds of dollars on the table. "That should cover everything. Since we're on a *break*, then I'll attend the events in Miami alone. That should give us both enough time to *think* about our relationship and decide if it's worth the hassle. Fair enough? Have a good night."

She marched toward the door.

"Dammit, Simone." Cameron went after her and slammed his palm on the door so she couldn't leave. "I haven't seen you in days. You don't have to leave."

She swung around, her face taut and angry. "Yes, I do. I have to leave because you're right, this isn't working. I have to think, too. If I want to deal with this. If I want everything I do for you to be picked apart. If I want to be accused of being something I'm not by someone who says he loves me. A snob. A bitch. Whatever it is you're thinking about me." Her voice cracked a little, but she took a deep breath and straightened her shoulders. "So yes, Cam, I have to go. Because we both have a lot to think about."

They stared at each other for a bit longer. Then, slowly, Cameron let his hand slide away.

Simone left and hauled the door closed, and it hit the doorframe with a thunderous clap that shook the walls and echoed in the loft.

In answer, Cameron slammed his hand against the wall and let out an angry roar of frustration.

Chapter Twenty

Simone left the podium to thunderous applause. Her speech summarizing the Johnson Foundation's accomplishments during the first quarter of the year was a big hit, confirming to donors and volunteers that the money was not only managed well, but spent on worthwhile causes.

She made her way toward the back of the ballroom, stopping every so often to shake hands and nod and pose for photographs. Eventually, she reached the double doors and exited into the hallway, away from the noise and din of the party. She slipped her phone from her purse and checked the screen. She'd received several phone calls, but none of them from Cameron.

She bit back her disappointment and smiled at a male donor as he went into the room, but the smile immediately disappeared once he was gone.

Tonight was a huge event, with plenty of media coverage. Upon arrival, wearing a crimson Oscar de la Renta flowing dress that left her arms and shoulders bare and looped around her neck in an asymmetrical design, Simone had done the obligatory twirl on the red carpet for photographers before joining her mother at their reserved table. The speeches were over, and the hired musicians played soft music in the background as guests talked and sipped champagne.

Normally, this was her element, but she felt unusually alone tonight.

Instead of wallowing in self-pity, she remembered the goals she intended to accomplish while in Miami. Over the next couple of days, she had important meetings scheduled, including one with representatives from a local children's organization to discuss how the Johnson Foundation could help them achieve their objective of ensuring that every child is healthy, housed, educated, and safe.

"Simone, what are you doing out here?"

Simone stiffened at the sound of her mother's voice.

She turned and faced Sylvie, whose tightly compressed lips effectively communicated her disapproval. Simone flashed a smile. "Hi, Mother."

Sylvie appeared the epitome of refinement, effecting a statuesque pose with one hand on her hip in black heels and a short-sleeved Chanel dress that skirted the floor. The décolleté gown offered a glimpse of cleavage and the belted waist showed off her trim figure, which rivaled women half her age. Her voluminous hair, even thicker and longer than Simone's, was piled into a tight but intricate design atop her head and held together with diamond-studded pins.

Simone tossed her phone into her clutch. "Did you need something?" she asked.

"One of the administrators for the children's hospital had questions I couldn't answer, so I came looking for you. You're the face of the foundation at this event, so it's important that you mingle and answer questions. You should not be sneaking off to have private conversations. I think that can wait, don't you?"

It was truly amazing how her mother could smile through any conversation. An onlooker would never guess that she was scolding her daughter.

The last thing Simone needed was for her mother to tell her how to do her job. She knew very well how to do her job, and did it well.

"Thank you for the advice. I'll keep it in mind."

"Is everything all right?" her mother asked.

Simone sighed and swallowed past the tightness in her throat. Staring at her purse, she said, "It's Cameron. We're on a break."

"Oh?"

"I bought him some gifts and he got very upset and basically let me know he didn't want anything from me. He started talking about how I was settling and he couldn't afford trips to the Amalfi—" Simone screeched to a halt and looked up at her mother. "Wait a minute, I never told him I took trips to the Amalfi Coast, yet somehow he knew."

"Oh?"

104

Simone's eyes widened. "*Mother.*"

"Simone—"

She took a couple of steps toward her mother. In a low voice, she asked, "*What did you do?*"

Sylvie's chin upticked and she sniffed, her face a portrait of complete unrepentance. "I simply went by to talk to the young man, to see where his head is. That's all."

Simone pressed a hand to her forehead. "That explains why he overreacted."

"Was it really an overreaction, or was that the truth? You can't hide from it, darling. If you want to get married, you must be with someone who understands you. Understands *us.*"

"You had no right to talk to him," Simone hissed. She could have choked her mother in that moment, but matricide was a crime.

Right then, her father strolled through the door, looking rather dapper in a tux, the loose curls on his head trimmed and tamed, with only a small swatch of gray near the front.

"I was looking for you." He held a bottle of the family's Full Moon beer in his right hand. His gaze flicked from Simone to her mother and back again, and he touched his free hand to her arm. "Everything all right?"

"Of course everything is all right, Oscar," Sylvie snapped, her mood immediately changed. Only with her ex-husband did Sylvie ever allow the cool mask of composure to slip. "Why wouldn't it be?"

Oh hell. This was the first time Simone had seen them together in years, and the enmity flaming between them hadn't diminished one iota.

"I was talking to my daughter." Oscar's eyes flicked over Sylvie, lingering a fraction too long at her breasts, before a muscle in his jaw flexed and he met her glowering stare with one of his own.

"Why don't you go back and entertain your lady friend?" Sylvie asked.

"My lady friend is fine without me."

"Really?" She examined her fingernails. "I wouldn't want her to feel out of place. It must be so confusing for someone of her age and profession to be thrust into such an environment. I'm sorry, what does she do again? She's a waitress or a hostess?" Sylvie actually sounded concerned, but they all knew better.

"It's none of your business what she does. The fact that she wasn't born with a silver spoon in her mouth is enough to make you prejudge her."

"I never prejudge. I make observations."

"You make assumptions based on your twisted world view."

"I draw conclusions based on past experience and observations. For instance, I observe that you wouldn't be here with your flavor of the month if you were never married to me. Thanks to a lovely settlement you can afford to hob knob with the rich and famous and pretend you're a lot more important so you can impress your teenaged girlfriend."

"She's not a teenager!" Oscar said, sounding appalled.

"Mother, please. Be nice for once." Listening to her parents quarrel was like being a child all over again.

Sylvie flashed her eyes at Simone. "Nice?" She returned her gaze to Oscar and her face hardened. "Why should I be nice, when your father is being so disrespectful to me? Did you have to bring your girlfriend here? Is this your way of trying to embarrass me?"

"For heaven's sake, Sylvie, the world doesn't revolve around you. I didn't even know you were coming this year until Simone told me. I had already bought the tickets."

"From now on, assume I'll be in attendance, and keep your adolescent girlfriends far away from me and this event." Sylvie tipped her chin higher. "Simone, I will see you inside. Please remember why you're here." She stalked off into the ballroom.

Oscar growled low in his throat and marched away from the door, his shoulders rigid with anger. Simone followed behind him.

He swung around and jabbed a hand toward the open door. "That woman is the devil. One of these days. One of these days..." He growled again and contracted his fingers into the universal sign of choking someone.

Oscar ran a hand over his hair, his khaki-colored skin flushed red with anger. "How are you doing?" he asked.

"Fine." Simone looped an arm through his and leaned on him. "Stop letting her get to you."

"Hard not to." He cursed under his breath. Letting out a puff of frustrated air, he ran a hand down his face, weathered from spending time out on his boat, one of his favorite pastimes.

"Can we talk for a bit? I need your advice. Let's sit." Simone steered him down the carpeted hall. "I can't believe you're drinking the family beer."

"Why not? It's good stuff." Her father shrugged. "I still eat at the pub occasionally, too, if you can believe that."

They stopped at an antique settee, and Simone lowered onto the floral fabric. Her father followed suit.

"What's on your mind?"

Simone crossed her legs. "I'm seeing someone. His name is Cameron and it's serious—or was, until right before I came here and he said he thought we should take a break."

"Let me guess. He doesn't have the right pedigree."

"Something like that."

"Does your mother know?"

"Unfortunately, I think she may have meddled and caused some of the problem."

Oscar shook his head in disgust. "How serious are you about this young man?"

"I'm in love with him," Simone said simply. "It happened fast, but I am." She launched into an explanation of how he'd reacted negatively to her gifts.

Oscar rested his elbows on his knees and turned in Simone's direction, letting the bottle of beer hang between his knees. "It's all well and good to take a break and think about your relationship, but it really sounds like the two of you need to talk. Get everything out into the open. All your hang ups and preconceived notions."

"I think you're right."

"I am right." He shot a sympathetic smile at her and patted her knee.

Even though Sylvie had gotten him riled up, her father looked relaxed in a way that Simone knew he never was when he and Sylvie were married.

Back then, Oscar expressed frustration and anger more often than not. Nowadays, he smiled a lot and laughed frequently—when Sylvie wasn't giving him hell.

"Did you ever love Mother?"

He stared across at the far wall for a few moments before he spoke. "Of course I loved her. I loved her when I married her." Oscar shifted to sit upright on the chair and took a swig from the bottle. "She wasn't always like that, but…something happened to her when her brother was murdered. She changed." One of Sylvie's brothers was the victim of a murder-suicide. "We argued constantly. It wasn't good for you kids to see us like that. I had to leave. Mentally, I left before the divorce, but when she brought it up, I was…relieved. I just no longer cared." He sighed and shook his head.

"If you loved her, why did you take a settlement?"

"Why not? I didn't want you kids living like bums when you came to see me. Besides I'd earned every dime of that settlement after all those years with that woman."

Simone bumped his shoulder and they both laughed softly.

As far as Simone knew, Oscar's settlement had ranged in the neighborhood of twenty-five to thirty million, but she didn't know the exact amount. The court documents were sealed, and no doubt more for her mother's benefit than her father's. Sylvie was embarrassed by the fact that she had not only lost a court battle with him but had been forced to settle and essentially pay him off to get rid of him.

"Your mother is incapable of being vulnerable enough to open herself up to love," Oscar said. "She thinks she has to be prepared at all times for someone who's going to take advantage of her, so rather than be taken advantage of, she presents this front of being strong. She pushes people away and then accuses them of leaving her." The last sentence came out edged with bitterness.

"Do you still love her?"

Oscar's head jerked up from studying the bottle of beer. "Your mother doesn't want to be loved."

He never actually answered the question, but she chose not to point out the avoidance. "Why did you leave us?" Simone asked quietly.

Oscar sighed. "I didn't want to leave you kids, but I got tired. I got tired of fighting and tired of not living up to her expectations, whatever those are. And I realized for my own sanity I needed to walk away because she would never be happy."

"Sometimes I think she misses you."

The comment was greeted with a bark of laughter.

"I'm serious," Simone said.

"You're delusional, but I forgive you because you're my daughter, and for a long time I was delusional, too. I thought that I could change your mother but I guess I simply was not strong enough to deal with her personality." He smiled in a sad, defeated way.

Simone rested her head on her father's shoulder. "So what should I do about Cameron?"

"What do you think you should do?"

"I'm asking you."

Oscar didn't speak for a while. When he did, he spoke in a quiet tone. "The two of you need to talk and figure out if your problems are insurmountable. Which they're not, by the way. The honeymoon is over and you're experiencing growing pains, that's all. You're two cultures clashing, and it's causing friction. But I understand where your young man is coming from. I experienced the same problem with your mother, and you have to understand, from a male point of view, it's tough when your woman is so much better off financially. You realize you can't keep up. You realize there's nothing you can offer that she can't get for herself, and then the question becomes, why does she need you?" He went silent for a long time, and Simone thought he was finished, but then he spoke again. "I felt that way with your mother, and it's hard when you feel as if you aren't good enough, and the person you love thinks you're not good enough. Whether real or imagined, that's a true emotion that can cause problems. In any relationship."

Simone lifted her head. "Is it really over between you and Mother?"

Oscar chuckled. "We've been divorced for fifteen years, and you saw what happened just now. We can barely tolerate each other." He drained the last of the beer and set the bottle on the floor.

"But maybe—"

"Why are you playing matchmaker all of a sudden?"

Simone shrugged. "You and Mother remind me of me and Cameron. I feel as if the two of you aren't finished."

"That's wishful thinking."

"But your relationship was perfect at one time. It was a long time ago, but I remember."

She recalled her father's playfulness and affection with her mother, and the adoring way her mother used to look at her father, as if there were no other man in the world for her.

"Perfect?" Oscar snorted. His gaze travelled up the hallway to the doorway Sylvie had disappeared into. "There's no such thing as a perfect relationship." He frowned thoughtfully, his eyes grave when he looked at Simone. "Relationships are either successful or unsuccessful, but they're never perfect. The successful ones…they're the ones where the couple never gives up."

Chapter Twenty-One

With the festivities at an end, Simone left the ballroom and passed through the lobby to the bank of elevators. Her first appointment wasn't until ten o'clock tomorrow morning, which meant she could sleep late if she wanted to. She had one more black tie event to attend tomorrow night, and then an appointment to tour the new surgery wing of the children's hospital the Johnson Foundation had funded. Then she was flying home.

She entered the elevator and nodded a greeting at the couple who joined her. Right before the doors closed, a set of big hands pried them apart and someone else slipped in.

Simone drew a sharp breath. "Cam."

He was wearing the tuxedo and shoes she'd bought and a grave expression on his face. "Hi."

Overwhelmed at first, Simone couldn't speak. Elation flooded her chest, and all she could do was stare. Finally, she managed to ask, "Why are you here?"

"You need an escort for the weekend, right?" he asked.

"Yes, but…" Her brow wrinkled. "You're late. The first event is over."

He ran a hand down the front of the tux. "I dressed the part before I left Atlanta, thinking as soon as I arrived I could come to the ballroom." He shook his head. "Flight delay."

"Oh."

The elevator stopped and Cameron stepped aside to allow the couple off, but his eyes didn't leave her.

"I missed you," he said softly as the elevator doors closed.

"I haven't been gone long."

"That's how bad it is."

They were quiet while the elevator ascended. When it arrived on her floor, they exited and walked in silence down the hallway. Simone was almost embarrassed to invite him into the plush suite the size of an apartment with a sitting room, kitchenette, and large bedroom. It confirmed what she suspected he thought—that she lived a life of excess.

The open drapes looked out onto Biscayne Bay, plunged in darkness at this time of night.

Simone set her purse beside the lamp on one of the tables. "Cam—"

"Before you say anything, hear me out." He took a deep breath and stuffed his hands into his pockets. "I've been doing a lot of thinking about you and me. We're different in a lot of ways. You like flash. I like simple. Even our work schedules seem to be conspiring against us. You work during the day. I work at night. I function off of five or six hours of sleep, you need a full eight or you're cranky and whiny."

"I'm not cranky and whiny."

"Yes, you are," he said, his mouth lifting at the corner. "The thing is, I worked hard to get where I am, and I'm proud of my accomplishments."

"As you should be."

His eyes became thoughtful as they looked into hers. "I can't afford the things you can, and I made the mistake of thinking that I would have to keep up, and if I couldn't, that was some kind of shortcoming."

"You don't have to keep up," Simone hastily confirmed. "I love you, Cam. Not because of what you can do for me, but because of the way you treat me. You spoil me with your words and your actions."

It was one thing to be told you were goddess, but quite another to be treated like one. Cameron treated her like goddess. He could intimidate with his size, but he was a caring, loving man. The kind who rubbed her feet after a long night networking in five-inch heels, and one who remembered little details, like she couldn't eat soy because she broke out in hives, and served her green tea with honey because she preferred it to sugar. She couldn't stand the thought of him treating another woman with the same care and tenderness.

"But I do have to wonder, are you sure you can be happy with me?" she asked. "I'm worried you'll resent me. I've been thinking, too, and I don't want to change. I realize the way I live can seem excessive, but I love my life and who I am."

Cameron didn't respond. Instead, with a hand to her spine, he led her to the sofa, where they both sat down. "I got a call from Brent, the furniture salesman, to thank me for the purchase. Said he wanted me to get a message to you and didn't know how to reach you personally. At first I thought, why the hell is he trying to talk to my woman? Then he explained that his daughter's situation didn't qualify for aid from the Johnson Foundation, but an anonymous donor flew her and his wife to Texas for the next round of surgery anyway, all expenses paid. The donor also paid the balance on their hospital bill. You did that, didn't you?"

Simone looked down at her hands. "It was nothing." Deeply moved by the story Brent shared, she'd paid for everything out of her own pocket.

Cameron took her hands in his. The warm clasp relaxed and comforted her.

"What you did is not nothing. Taking care of all their expenses is huge. You've never asked me to change who I am, and I don't want you to change. I love who you are. You're generous, and that's why you're so good at what you do. Your family knows that and chose you to be the foundation's ambassador because you're thoughtful and pay attention to people's needs. And me...I'm an ass who is way too sensitive."

"You are a bit of an ass." She smiled at him. "But I learned something about myself tonight. Something I hadn't considered until I saw my parents together."

"Your parents actually talked to each other?"

"Barely, and somehow managed not to kill each other." They both laughed. "I tested you, without realizing it."

He frowned. "Tested me how?"

Simone took a deep breath. "My mother, Ella, and I think that maybe we're cursed or something, and the only way to be truly happy is to find a man who is just as wealthy as we are. My father was not wealthy, and he left my mother. My brother-in-law was not wealthy, and he left my sister. When you reacted so negatively about the clothes I bought, an alarm went off in my head. I wanted to buy you the furniture because you're always so good to me, and

I wanted to do something for you—to show you how much I love and appreciate you. But I hesitated, wondering how you'd react. Then, I did it. I didn't realize it at the time, but it was a test, and you reacted the way that I'd feared."

Cameron nodded slowly. "Not one of my finer moments. I was upset, but you can't get rid of me that easily. I'm not going anywhere." He held up his wrists, displaying the cufflinks she'd bought. "How else will I be able to show off twelve hundred dollar dinosaur cufflinks, but at events you and I attend?"

"Cam..."

He grinned, that sexy smile from his beautiful lips. "I'm sorry, sweetheart. This is the last time I'll mention them, but you know this is some crazy shit, right?"

She pouted.

"But I can get used to it," he said softly. "I'm looking forward to learning to ski and taking a ski trip to Italy. I want to see the hidden valley you told me about."

"It's beautiful."

He cupped her face, bringing his mouth within inches of hers. "Not as beautiful as you, I bet." He kissed her.

"Mmm," Simone murmured, pulling back and resting a hand on his chest. "Before we get carried away, we need to talk about my mother. I know she came to see you."

"She did," he confirmed with a nod.

"Whatever she said, ignore her," Simone said firmly. "She does not speak for me."

Cameron chuckled. "I realize that, but for a second..." He shook his head with regret. "I let her get inside my head. Now that I know better, I'm looking forward to a trip to the Amalfi Coast."

"It's gorgeous. You'll love it," Simone promised.

Cameron pulled her onto his lap. "Man, I missed you," he murmured.

He pressed his mouth harder against hers, and Simone moaned, spreading her fingers out across his chest. Cameron showered affection on her lips, neck, and the neckline of the dress.

His fingers found the long split, and he cursed, pushing the filmy material off her leg so he could touch her bare thigh. "Look at you," he murmured.

After a few more kisses, they made their way into the adjoining bedroom. Simone kicked off her heels and he undressed her with care, interrupting the removal of each article of clothing with kisses each time more naked flesh became uncovered.

Simone removed his clothes, and caressed his neck and shoulders, and dragged her tongue along his muscular chest. They lowered onto the bed, and before long, he was inside her. They groaned and gasped at the same time when he moved, their voices mingling so perfectly they sounded like one. He thrust deep and slow, all the way to the base each time, and she savored the sensation of each penetrating movement of his hips.

His groans of pleasure crashed into her eardrums every time he lunged between her open legs, and when her climax came, it was powerful and all-consuming. Helplessly, Simone clung to him. Satisfied. Relieved. Content.

"Hey." Cameron cupped her face and kissed her cheek, the corner of her mouth, and her chin.

She didn't even realize she was crying until his thumbs brushed the tears from the corners of her eyes.

"I love you," she said.

His gaze held hers. "I love you, too. I'll always love you."

"I hate it when we fight," she whispered brokenly.

"Then let's not fight anymore."

He pulled her into his arms, and Simone nestled her face into his neck, more tears seeping from her eyes and dampening his skin. They lay there for an indeterminate amount of time, wrapped in each other's arms.

Just...holding on.

Epilogue

The VIP section on the mezzanine level of Club Masquerade offered a good view of the dance floor. Simone looked down at the bumping and grinding bodies below. Nearby, Ella sat on a white chair, texting rapidly. Meanwhile Stephan and Reese huddled on a white sectional with a duo of women they'd plucked from downstairs to keep them company.

Harper and Mason came in, and Simone rushed over to them. "Where's Cam?" she asked.

"He should be along any minute now," Harper replied, an odd smile on her face. As if she were hiding something.

Simone sighed and went back to the railing, a bit annoyed at Cameron's tardiness. He never kept her waiting. He'd promised if she met him here, he'd leave early and they'd go back to his place for a quiet evening.

The past year had flown by, during which so many changes had taken place. After Cameron, Simone, and Sylvie ate lunch together one day, during which Cameron declared his love for Simone and made it clear that he had no intention of going anywhere or hurting her, Sylvie finally set aside her reservations about their relationship. Over time, she warmed up to him enough that she often insisted he join them for social engagements.

At the same time, Simone had become close with Harper and Mason. She joined Cameron in the tradition of cooking meals for them at his home, and the group had expanded to six, which included Harper's fiancé, Hunter, and Mason's wife, London.

All of a sudden, the music in the entire venue stopped, and the crowd moaned and cried out their discontent.

"Can I have your attention please," the deejay hollered. "Ladies and gentlemen, we have a big announcement to make at the club tonight. But I won't be making that announcement. One of the owners, Cameron Bennett, has something to say."

Simone glanced over at Harper and Mason, both of whom smiled at her. When their gazes shifted to a point over her shoulder, she swung around to see Cameron coming toward her with a microphone and a spotlight trained on him. Devastatingly handsome in a blue jacket, black shirt, and black tie, he took her breath away.

"What is going on?" Simone asked no one in particular. Her pulse tripped over itself in excitement.

Cameron spoke into the mic but kept his eyes on her. "This is highly unusual, but I wanted to introduce you all to the woman I love."

As high-pitched whistles and cheers went up from the crowd, Simone's pulse beat even faster. He was smiling, but there was an intense look to his eyes.

He continued speaking. "Over a year ago, Simone Brooks came into my life, and tonight I brought her back to the place where we met to ask a very important question."

He lowered to one knee and the crowd went wild. Simone took a step back and slapped a hand over her open mouth.

Love shining in his eyes for everyone to see, Cameron continued. "From the first night I met you, I knew you were special, and you changed my life in so many ways. Now I understand why none of my other relationships worked. I was waiting for you. And because of you, I wake up every morning with a smile on my face. Simone Brooks, would you do me the honor and privilege of becoming my wife?" He extended a black velvet box with a radiant cut diamond nestled in black satin.

The ring was huge. He must have spent a fortune to get her a stone that large, and because of his conservative nature, she appreciated it even more. It was exactly the kind of ring she wanted. He knew her so well.

Simone nodded immediately, mutely, and the crowd went wild. Their siblings shouted their approval, and a big grin spread across Cameron's indecently beautiful lips.

"Yes, yes, yes!" Simone whispered, rushing over and clutching his face. Her hair cascaded around them as she kissed him fully and thoroughly on the mouth to more cheers and whistles.

Cameron slipped the ring on her trembling finger and then stood, lifting her off her feet. Laughing, her heart full and happier than she could ever remember, Simone took the mic. "He's all mine, ladies!" she screamed.

A roar of laughter and more cheering filled the venue.

As the music started again, Cameron's eyes smiled into hers. "Love you, sweetheart. Forever and always."

"I love you, too. Forever. And always," Simone whispered.

Unable to help themselves, they sealed the promise with one more kiss.

The Bennett Triplets

Buy the other books in the series to read a love match for Cameron's siblings!

A Passionate Night by Candace Shaw

Mixing business with pleasure leads to a passionate night...

Harper Bennett's motto is work hard, play hard. Lately, she's forgotten the latter and has focused her time as part-owner, along with her brothers, of the hottest nightclub in Atlanta. When an intriguing client enters, Harper forgoes her promise to never date a man that doesn't live in the same city and she finds herself playing hard to get with Hunter Arrington. The passion that has ignited between them can't be extinguished, and she dreads the day he has to leave.

Hunter travels the world because of his career and has no intentions of settling down until his eyes land on Harper. There's something about the petite, sassy woman that he adores and makes him feel at home for the first time in years. Now he's faced with a life-changing decision and the thought of being without Harper isn't an option.

A Passionate Kiss by Sharon C. Cooper

Retired Marine, Mason Bennett, has two goals: adjust to civilian life and keep drama out of it. His focus is on his role as part-owner, along with his siblings, of Atlanta's hottest nightclub. However, his attention shifts when the woman he has loved like a sister reenters his life and thoughts of a passionate kiss they shared hijacks his mind. Their connection is explosive. Feelings he's tried to deny come to the forefront, and he's tempted to do something he thought he would never do—cross that line from friends to lovers.

TV news anchor, London Alexander, is back home in Atlanta and ready to start a new chapter in her life. This time she hopes her future includes Mason, the man she has loved forever. She's ready to step over the forbidden line that he's drawn in their relationship.

Will taking a chance on love lead to a happily-ever-after? Or will risking their friendship leave them both with broken hearts?

Johnson Family series

If you enjoyed *A Passionate Love*, check out my series about Simone's cousins, the Johnson Family—a billionaire beer and restaurant dynasty based in Seattle. Meet Lucas and Ivy, Cyrus and Daniella, Trenton and Alannah, Gavin and Terri, and coming soon…a love match for Xavier.

BUY THE SERIES AT ALL MAJOR ONLINE RETAILERS

More Stories by Delaney Diamond

Love Unexpected series
The Blind Date
The Wrong Man
An Unexpected Attraction
The Right Time
One of the Guys
That Time in Venice (coming soon)

Johnson Family series
Unforgettable
Perfect
Just Friends
The Rules
Good Behavior (coming soon)

Hot Latin Men series
The Arrangement
Fight for Love
Private Acts
The Ultimate Merger
Second Chances
More Than a Mistress (coming soon)
Hot Latin Men: Vol. I (print anthology)
Hot Latin Men: Vol. II (print anthology)

Hawthorne Family series
The Temptation of a Good Man
A Hard Man to Love
Here Comes Trouble
For Better or Worse
Hawthorne Family Series: Vol. I (print anthology)
Hawthorne Family Series: Vol. II (print anthology)

Bailar series (sweet/clean romance)
Worth Waiting For

Stand Alones
Still in Love
Subordinate Position
Heartbreak in Rio (part of Endless Summer Nights)

Free Stories
www.delaneydiamond.com

About The Author

Delaney Diamond is the USA Today Bestselling Author of sweet, sensual, passionate romance novels. Originally from the U.S. Virgin Islands, she now lives in Atlanta, Georgia. She reads romance novels, mysteries, thrillers, and a fair amount of nonfiction. When she's not busy reading or writing, she's in the kitchen trying out new recipes, dining at one of her favorite restaurants, or traveling to an interesting locale. She speaks fluent conversational French and can get by in Spanish.

Enjoy free reads and the first chapter of all her novels on her website. Join her mailing list to get sneak peeks, notices of sale prices, and find out about new releases.

www.delaneydiamond.com

Made in the USA
Middletown, DE
20 July 2018